Growing Up

RACHEL YODER—
Always Trouble Somewhere

Book 8

Growing Up

RACHEL YODER—
Always Trouble Somewhere

Book 8

WANDA &
BRUNSTETTER

BARBOUR
PUBLISHING

Published by Barbour Publishing, Inc., P.O. Box 719, Uhrichsville, Ohio 44683, www.barbourbooks.com

Our mission is to publish and distribute inspirational products offering exceptional value and biblical encouragement to the masses.

Member of the
Evangelical Christian
Publishers Association

Printed in the United States of America.

Dickinson Press Inc., Grand Rapids, MI; Print Code D10002202; February 2010

Dedication and Acknowledgments

To my six special grandchildren: Jinell, Ric, Madolynne, Rebekah, Philip, and Richelle. Though in different ways, you've each been an inspiration for the books in this series.

A special thanks goes to Richelle Brunstetter, Elvera Kienbaum, Richard Brunstetter Sr., Jean Brunstetter, Lorine VanCorbach, Leeann Curtis, and Jake Smucker for sharing some of their interesting stories with me. Thanks also to my editor, Kelly Williams, for allowing me to write this enjoyable children's series.

Glossary

absatz—stop
ach—oh
aldi—girlfriend
appenditlich—delicious
baremlich—terrible
bensel—silly child
bett—bed
Biewel—Bible
bletsching—spanking
boppli—baby
brieder—brothers
bruder—brother
buch—book
bussli—kitten
buwe—boy
daed—dad
danki—thanks
dumm—dumb
dummkopp—dunce
fraa—wife
gut—good
hinkel—chickens
hund—dog
hungerich—hungry
jah—yes
kapp—cap
katz—cat
koppweh—headache
kumme—come
mamm—mom

naas—nose
nodel—needle
sau—pig
schliffer—splinter
schnell—quickly
schpell—pin
umgerennt—upset
windel—diaper

Alli mudder muss sariye fer ihre famiyle.
Every mother has to take care of her family.

Die Rachel is die ganz zeit am grummle.
Rachel is grumbling all the time.

Er hot mich verschwetzt.
He talked me into it.

Es fenschder muss mer nass mache fer es sauwer mache.
One has to wet the window in order to clean it.

Ferwas bischt allfat so schtarkeppich?
Why are you always so stubborn?

Guder mariye.
Good morning.

Gut nacht.
Good night.

Hoscht du schunn geese?
Have you already eaten?

Was in der welt?
What in all the world?

Wie geht's?
How are you?

Windle wesche gleich ich net.
I don't like to wash out diapers.

Contents

Chapter 1
Sidetracked

"Ha! Ha! I beat you home!" Rachel Yoder shouted as she raced into the yard ahead of her brother Jacob.

"Grow up, Rachel," Jacob said when he caught up to her. "It doesn't matter who got to the house first."

"*Jah* [Yes], it does!" Rachel bounded up the porch steps. She didn't tell Jacob, but she figured if she got to the kitchen before he did, she'd get first pick of whatever snack Mom had waiting for them. If Jacob got there before she did, he'd probably eat more than his share and leave her with just a few crumbs.

Rachel jerked open the back door and rushed inside. She dropped her backpack in the utility room and raced into the kitchen. Her brows puckered when she saw that no snack was on the table. She glanced around. No food was waiting on the kitchen counter, either.

Rachel scratched the side of her head. "Now that's sure strange."

"What's strange?" Jacob asked, stepping into the room.

"Mom's not in the kitchen, and no snack is here for us."

"Maybe she's in her room with the *boppli* [baby]." Jacob took off his straw hat and hung it on a wall peg near the door. "We're not helpless, Rachel. We can get our own snacks, you know."

Rachel shook her head. "What if we eat something Mom doesn't want us to eat? What if we eat something she's planning to serve for supper? We'd be in trouble if we did that, and you know it."

Jacob grabbed an apple from the fruit bowl sitting on the counter. "I'm sure Mom won't care if we have a piece of fruit."

"No, I suppose not." Rachel took a banana and headed for the back door.

"Where are you going?" Jacob asked.

"Out to the greenhouse to help Grandpa!" Rachel called over her shoulder.

"Don't you think you'd better do your homework and get your chores done first?"

Rachel shook her head and kept walking. She could do those things later on.

Rachel found Grandpa in the greenhouse, snipping the leaves of a large leafy plant. "*Wie geht's* [How are you]?" she asked.

"I'm good. How was school?"

"It was okay, but I'm glad to be home. I was anxious to get here and work with you. It's a lot more fun than being in school."

"I'm always glad to have your help in our little greenhouse," Grandpa said.

Rachel smiled. She felt good to hear Grandpa refer to the greenhouse as *ours* and not *his*. "Have you had many customers today?" she asked.

He nodded. "This morning I was so busy I could hardly keep up. The business has slowed down a little this afternoon, though."

"I'll be glad when I've graduated from school and can be here all day to help you," Rachel said.

He nodded. "That will be nice, but in the meantime, you need to study hard and learn all you can while you are in school."

"I know." Rachel glanced around. "What do you need my help with today?"

"I was planning to fertilize some plants but haven't gotten around to it yet." Grandpa motioned to a shelf full of geraniums across the room. "You can do that now if you like."

"Sure, Grandpa." Rachel had fertilized plants before, so she knew just what to do. She hurried to the back room and took out the bottle of liquid fertilizer. She squeezed several drops into a jug of warm water, carried it into the other room, and began the process of fertilizing the plants. She'd only gotten a few of them done when the bell above the greenhouse door jingled and Mom stepped in. Her forehead was wrinkled and she didn't look one bit happy.

"Jacob said you didn't do your homework or any of your chores before you came out here," she said, peering at Rachel over the top of her metal-framed glasses.

Rachel swallowed hard. "I—uh—was planning to do them later—after I finished helping Grandpa in the greenhouse."

Mom slowly shook her head. "You know you're not supposed to come out here until your homework and chores are done. When are you going to grow up and start acting more responsible, Rachel?"

Rachel's cheeks felt like they were on fire as she stared at the floor and struggled not to cry. She didn't like it when Mom scolded her. It made her feel like a baby. "I—I just like being here so much, and I—"

"I know you like being here." Mom's voice softened a bit. She touched Rachel's chin, raising it so Rachel could look at her face. "However, schoolwork and chores come first. After those things are done, you can work in the greenhouse. Is that clear?"

"Jah," Rachel mumbled.

"What was that?"

"I said, 'Jah,' Mom."

Grandpa stepped forward. "Rachel was in the

middle of fertilizing some plants for me, Miriam. Is it all right if she finishes them and then goes up to the house?"

Mom nodded. Then she turned to Rachel and said, "Oh, by the way, I was changing your little sister's *windel* [diaper] when you and Jacob got home from school, so that's why there was no snack waiting for you. You can have some cookies and milk while you do your homework."

Rachel shook her head as she poured fertilizer onto another plant. "I ate a banana while I was walking out to the greenhouse, so I'm not really hungry."

Mom turned toward the door. "All right then. I'll expect to see you at the house in a few minutes." She stepped out of the greenhouse, and the bell above the door jingled when the door closed behind her.

"I guess I should have asked if you'd done your homework and chores before I put you to work out here," Grandpa said to Rachel. "Next time, I will ask."

Tears burned the backs of Rachel's eyes. Grandpa didn't trust her anymore. He probably thought she was a baby, too. "I like working for you in the greenhouse more than doing chores or homework," she said.

Grandpa touched Rachel's shoulder. "I'm sure you do, but there's one thing you should always remember."

"What's that?"

"The Bible teaches us to do whatever we do as if we are doing it for the Lord," Grandpa said.

"Really?"

Grandpa nodded. "If you remember that, you will find it easier to do the things you don't enjoy so much."

Rachel smiled, wondering if she'd ever be as smart as Grandpa.

When Rachel returned to the house, she found Mom peeling potatoes at the kitchen sink.

"Is it time to start supper already?" Rachel asked.

Mom shook her head. "Not quite, but your little sister might wake up from her nap soon, and then I'll be busy feeding her. So I thought it would be a good idea if I started preparing supper early." She glanced at Rachel over her shoulder. "It's always good to stay ahead of things."

Rachel nodded. "Should I do my homework first or start on my chores?"

"You'd better do your chores first. Now that summer's over, it gets dark earlier than before."

"Okay. What chores do you want me to do?" Rachel asked.

"Let's see now. . . . Jacob is cleaning the chicken coop, which I was going to ask you to do before you went out to the greenhouse."

Rachel wrinkled her nose. Cleaning the smelly chicken coop was not her favorite thing to do. She was glad Jacob had been asked to do it this time.

Mom held the potato peeler out to Rachel. "If you'd rather do an inside chore, you can finish peeling the potatoes, while I take the dry clothes off the line."

Rachel frowned. The last time she'd peeled potatoes she had nicked her finger. "I'd rather get the clothes," she mumbled.

Mom nodded. "The laundry basket's sitting on the back porch."

Rachel scurried out the door, picked up the basket, and hurried out to the clothesline. Several big fluffy towels flapped in the breeze, along with some of the men's trousers and a few dresses. There were also lots of baby diapers and some little outfits that her three-month-old sister, Hannah, wore.

Rachel set the basket on the wagon she often used to haul laundry to and from the house. Then she stood on her tiptoes, yanked the clothespins free, and dropped the towels into the basket. She was about to remove one of the clothespins from a pair of Grandpa's trousers when Cuddles leaped into the basket. *Meow!*

Rachel giggled and bent down to rub her cat's head. "You silly *katz* [cat]. What do you think you're doing?"

Purr. . .purr. . .purr. Cuddles nuzzled Rachel's fingers with her warm pink nose.

Rachel took a seat on the ground and put the cat in her lap. Cuddles purred louder as Rachel stroked behind the cat's ears.

Just then Cuddles's kitten, Snowball, zipped across the yard, leaped into the air, and landed on Cuddles's head.

Yeow! Cuddles jumped up as if she had springs on her legs, and then tore across the yard, hissing and meowing as she raced to the barn.

Snowball burrowed into Rachel's lap and began to purr.

"Shame on you for chasing your *mamm* [mom] away." Rachel shook her finger at Snowball.

The cat only purred louder and licked Rachel's hand with a sandpapery tongue.

Rachel smiled. Snowball was spoiled, no doubt about it, and she liked lots of attention.

Neigh! Neigh! Rachel looked over her shoulder and saw Tom, their old retired buggy horse, with his head hanging over the fence. *Neigh! Neigh!* Tom bobbed his head up and down and opened his mouth very wide.

Rachel chuckled. "I'll bet you'd like an apple, wouldn't you, Tom?"

Neigh! Neigh!

"Oh, all right. I'll go inside and get you one." Rachel set Snowball on the ground and sprinted for the house.

Mom wasn't in the kitchen, and Rachel figured she must be in her room with the baby. She hurried to the fruit bowl and grabbed a big red apple; then she rushed back outside.

Old Tom stuck his head out even farther as Rachel

approached the fence. As soon as she opened the gate and stepped into the pasture, Tom plodded over and nudged her arm with his nose.

Rachel snickered. "Okay, okay. Don't be in such a hurry." She placed the apple in the palm of her hand and held it out to him.

Old Tom lowered his head. *Crunch! Crunch! Slurp! Slurp!* He took his time eating the apple and drooled a lot. When he was done, he nudged Rachel's arm with his nose again.

"Sorry, Tom, but I only brought one apple for you." Rachel patted Tom's flank. "You're such a good horse. I'm glad Pap put you out to pasture when you got too old to pull the buggy. I would have been sad if Pap had sold you to the glue factory, like Jacob said he might do."

Tom wandered over to a tree, dropped to his knees, and rolled onto his side. Then he reached down and out with his mouth, as though he was yawning, and let out a strange-sounding sigh. Just seeing him there made Rachel feel tired.

She leaned against the fence and closed her eyes, letting her mind wander. She thought about the letter she'd received from her cousin Mary a few weeks ago. Mary had let Rachel know that she'd made it safely home. Rachel had fun when Mary had come for a visit. She couldn't wait to visit Mary in Indiana someday.

Rachel thought about the bonfire Pap said he

might build Saturday evening. They'd probably roast hot dogs and marshmallows and enjoy plenty of freshly squeezed apple cider. Rachel's sister Esther and her husband, Rudy, would be invited, too.

"Rachel! Where are you?"

Rachel turned and saw Mom standing on the porch. "I'm coming," she called.

Rachel hurried out of the pasture and ran all the way to the house. "I'm here," she said breathlessly as she stepped onto the porch.

Mom gave Rachel a curious look over the top of her glasses. "Where's the basket of clothes?"

"Huh?"

"The clothes, Rachel." Mom pursed her lips. "I sent you to get the clothes off the line some time ago, remember?"

Rachel reached under her stiff white *kapp* [cap] and scratched her head. "Oh yeah, that's right. Guess I lost track of what I was doing."

"What *have* you been doing all this time?" Mom asked, giving Rachel a stern look.

Rachel shifted from one foot to the other, feeling like a fly trapped in a spider's web. "Well, I—uh—"

"Did you take any of the clothes off the line?"

"Jah. Well, part of them, anyway."

Tap! Tap! Tap! Mom's foot beat on the porch and she folded her arms. "If you only got part of the clothes, then what were you doing the rest of the time? And where are the clothes you took off the line?"

"Uh—some are still on the line. The others are in the basket."

Tap! Tap! Tap! "Why didn't you take all the clothes off the line, Rachel?"

"I—uh—got distracted."

"Distracted by what?"

Rachel held up one finger. "First Cuddles landed in the basket of clothes." A second finger came up. "Then Snowball came along and jumped on Cuddles's head." Rachel lifted a third finger. "Then Old Tom came over begging for an apple, so I—"

Mom held up her hand. "You became sidetracked?"

Rachel nodded. "I just wanted to have a little fun, and—"

"No excuses, Rachel. When a person's asked to do a job, he or she should do it." Mom pointed to the clothesline. "I want you to finish the job I asked you to do, right now."

"Okay, Mom." Rachel trudged to the clothesline. One by one she quickly removed the wooden pins holding the men's trousers. She put the trousers in the basket. Then she took down the dresses, diapers, and baby clothes.

Chirp-or-ee! Chirp-or-ee! A bird called from a nearby tree.

Rachel was tempted to sit on the grass and watch the bird but knew she'd be in trouble if she did. With a heavy sigh, she grabbed the wagon handle and pulled it to the house. She wished she didn't have any chores to do!

As Rachel helped Mom fold clothes at the foot of Mom's bed, she thought about Grandpa's greenhouse.

I'd rather be out there! she thought. It was a lot more fun to water, repot, and prune plants than it was to fold Hannah's diapers.

She glanced at her baby sister, lying in the crib on the other side of Mom and Pap's room, and wondered when Esther's baby would be born. Would it be a boy or a girl? Would it have blond hair or brown? What color would the baby's eyes be?

Mom nudged Rachel's arm. "Watch what you're doing, Rachel. You're folding that windel the wrong way."

Rachel looked down at the pile of diapers still on the bed and frowned. "I don't like doing this. It's boring."

"Why don't you make a game out of your chores, the way Grandpa taught you to do several months ago?" Mom's glasses had slipped to the end of her nose, and she paused to push them back in place. "I'm sure you can think of something to pretend while you're helping me fold clothes."

Rachel nibbled on her lower lip as she tried to think of something fun about folding diapers. She couldn't think of a thing!

Moo! Moo! Stomp! Stomp! Stomp!

"Now what's going on outside?" Mom hurried to the window and peered out. "*Ach* [Oh] no! The cows are out of the pasture! They're running all over our yard!"

She rushed out of the room, calling over her shoulder, "*Kumme* [Come], Rachel, *schnell* [quickly]. Help me get the cows back in the pasture!"

Rachel followed Mom down the hall and out the back door. When they stepped into the yard, Mom raised her hands and shouted, "Just look at my garden! They've trampled everything to the ground!"

Rachel dashed into the yard and shooed a cow toward the pasture. Soon the other cows followed.

"Look there," said Mom, pointing her finger. "The pasture gate's wide open!" She turned and looked at Rachel sternly. "Did you open that gate, Rachel?"

Rachel quickly closed the gate behind the last cow. She turned to Mom and said, "I opened it when I went to give old Tom an apple. Guess I must have gotten sidetracked and forgot to close it when I left."

Mom shook her head. "You've gotten sidetracked way too much this afternoon, Rachel. Now you'll have double chores to do for the next few days."

Rachel frowned. "Can't I just help you replant the garden?"

"It's too late in the season for that. Maybe a

few extra chores will help you remember not to get sidetracked the next time you're asked to do something." Mom turned and went back into the house.

Rachel swallowed around the lump in her throat. She couldn't believe she'd already forgotten what Grandpa had said about doing her chores as if she was doing them for the Lord. Wouldn't she ever grow up?

Chapter 2

Too Many Chores

For the last half hour, Rachel had been sitting at the kitchen table with her notepaper, a pencil, and a stack of books. She was supposed to do her homework, but it was a lot more fun to look at the book about a cat that she had borrowed from the book mobile. The book mobile was like a traveling library that frequently came to the Amish community. Rachel had done some of her homework, but not all of it. She planned to finish it sometime before going to bed.

"Rachel, are you done with your homework?" Mom asked as she ran water into the kitchen sink.

Rachel glanced at her schoolbooks then at the cat book. "Uh—jah, I'm just about done."

"That's good, because it's time for you to do the supper dishes," Mom said.

Rachel groaned. "Already?"

Mom nodded. "I want you to wash and dry them all, and then I have some mending for you to do."

Rachel frowned. "What about Jacob? Isn't he helping with the dishes?"

Mom shook her head. "Part of your punishment for leaving the pasture gate open is doing extra chores, remember?"

Rachel nodded slowly as a lump formed in her throat. She didn't think it was fair that Jacob didn't have to help with the dishes just because she had extra chores. Why should he have the evening free to do as he pleased?

"The sink's ready for you now, Rachel. Are you coming?" Mom peered at Rachel over the top of her glasses.

"I'll be there in a minute."

Waaa! Waaa! Waaa!

"I'm going to check on Hannah. Now you get busy on those dishes," Mom said as she scurried out of the room.

"I wish I didn't have to work all the time," Rachel mumbled. "I wish I was a katz. They don't have any chores to do. They get to lie around and sleep all day or scamper everywhere, having all sorts of fun. Jah, I wish I was a katz."

"Why do you wish you were a cat?" asked Rachel's oldest brother, Henry, when he entered the kitchen.

"Cats have life so easy," Rachel explained.

"You think so, huh?" Henry tapped Rachel lightly on the head. "Think about it, little sister. Your cats get chased by Jacob's dog, and they have to look for warm spots to sleep on cold days. They can also get worms from eating too many birds and mice, and they often get hair balls." He tapped her head one more time. "And another thing—cats can't read books! Now do you think those furry critters have it so well?"

She shrugged. "At least they don't have to do dishes."

Henry chuckled, poured himself a cup of coffee, and left the room.

Rachel banged her book shut and jumped out of the chair. "I may as well get this over with!"

Rachel grabbed the sponge and dropped it into the soapy water. Then she picked up a dish and sloshed the sponge over it. Next, she rinsed the dish and placed it in the dish drainer.

The dishwater was beginning to cool, so Rachel turned on the hot water. She turned on a little more cold water so she wouldn't burn her hands. While the sink was filling, she stared out the window and daydreamed about how much fun she'd have if she ever visited Mary in Indiana and went to the Fun Spot Amusement Park.

"Rachel, are you almost done with the dishes?" Mom called from the other room. "And don't forget, you still have to mend some things before you go to bed."

"I'll be done soon," Rachel hollered. She grabbed another plate to wash and realized that she'd filled the sink too full. Water had begun running onto the floor.

"Oh no," she mumbled as she turned off the water. She grabbed a towel, dropped to her knees, and mopped up the spot where the water had puddled.

I need to concentrate on what I'm doing, she told herself as she began washing dishes again.

Whoosh!—a bubble flew up and popped on Rachel's chin. It made her wish this was a warm summer day and that she could be outside blowing bubbles with her bubble wand. But no, she was stuck in here, doing dirty dishes in a hot, stuffy kitchen!

By the time Rachel had finished washing the dishes, she was tired, bored, and not in the mood to dry the dishes. However, she knew if she left them in the dish drainer, she'd be in more trouble with Mom. Besides, she remembered she was supposed to be doing her chores for the Lord.

Rachel picked up a glass and dried it with a clean towel. She was about to set it on the counter when— *bam!*—the back door hit the wall as it swung open.

Rachel was so startled when Jacob entered the room that the glass slipped from her hands and fell to the floor. *Crash!* Her hand shook as she pointed to the broken glass. "Look what you made me do!" she shouted at Jacob.

He shook his head and raised his hands. "Don't blame me. You did that yourself."

"If you hadn't slammed the door and scared me, I

wouldn't have dropped the glass."

"Grow up, little *bensel* [silly child], and quit blaming others for things you've caused yourself."

Rachel shook her finger at Jacob. "Stop calling me a silly child!"

"I will when you stop acting like one." He grabbed an apple from the fruit bowl on the counter and sauntered out of the room.

Rachel's chin quivered, and her eyes filled with tears as she squatted to pick up the broken glass. "Jacob Yoder, you're a mean boy," she muttered under her breath.

By the time Rachel had cleaned up the broken glass and finished drying the dishes, she'd forgotten that Mom had asked her to do mending. She grabbed her cat book and headed up the stairs.

"Where are you going, Rachel?" Mom called from the living room.

Rachel halted on the steps and turned around. She knew right then what she'd forgotten. "I'll be there in a few minutes," she called to Mom. "I'm taking my book upstairs to my room."

When Rachel entered the living room a few minutes later, she found Grandpa sitting in the rocking chair in front of the fireplace, holding Hannah. Pap and Henry sat at a small table on the other side of the room, playing a game of checkers. Jacob stood behind Henry, watching over his shoulder. Mom sat on the sofa with a basket of mending in her lap.

"Kumme," Mom said, motioning Rachel over to the sofa. "One of your dresses needs the hem let down."

Rachel grunted as she flopped down beside Mom. "You know I'm not good at sewing."

Mom handed Rachel the small metal seam ripper. "The more you do, the better you'll get."

"That's right," Grandpa spoke up. "Practice makes perfect."

Rachel wrinkled her nose. "I don't think I'll ever be perfect at sewing, no matter how much practicing I do."

Mom reached over and patted Rachel's arm. "Just do your best."

Rachel squinted as she picked at the threads in the hem of her dress. "This is what I get for growing so much this summer," she mumbled.

"What was that?" Mom asked.

"Oh, nothing."

"King me!" Pap hollered from across the room, where he and Henry were playing checkers.

"I sure didn't see that coming," Henry said with a groan.

Jacob nudged Henry's shoulder. "Then you oughta pay closer attention to the game."

Henry scowled at Jacob. "Why don't you find something else to do and quit bothering me? I can't concentrate with you hovering around."

"I'm not hovering. I'm keeping my eye on the game, because I'll get to play whoever wins."

Rachel smiled. As much as she didn't like sewing, she'd rather be doing that than playing checkers with Jacob. He didn't play fair and always tried to distract her so he would win. She sometimes got frustrated and quit before the game was over, but the last time they'd played checkers, she'd let Jacob win just so he'd quit bothering her.

"I'm done ripping out the hem," Rachel said, handing the dress to Mom.

"Now you need to make a new hem." Mom handed Rachel a container of pins, a needle, and some dark green thread.

"How am I supposed to know how big I should make the hem?" Rachel questioned.

"Let's see now. . . ." Mom gave her chin a couple of taps. "You grew two inches over the summer, and you'll need to allow for more growth that might occur during this school year." She handed Rachel a measuring tape. "I would suggest that you make the hem on your dress three inches longer than it used to be."

Rachel frowned. This would take a lot longer than she'd expected.

Mom looked at Rachel again. "Once you've got the hem turned up, you'll need to thread your needle and sew it in place. Oh, and be sure you make tiny stitches so the thread doesn't show too much."

This isn't fair, Rachel thought. *At this rate, I'll be here all night!*

"Another king for me!" Pap shouted as he clapped his hands.

Rachel jumped and stuck herself with a pin. "Ouch!"

"What's wrong?" Mom asked with a look of concern.

"When I heard Pap holler, I jammed a *schpell* [pin] into my finger." Rachel stuck her finger in her mouth and sucked on it. The metallic taste of blood made her lips pucker as she scrunched up her nose. "I'm bleeding, Mom. I don't think I can finish this dress tonight."

"Let me see."

Rachel held her hand out to Mom. "It really stings."

"It always stings whenever I prick my finger," Mom said, "but it never lasts long. Just blow on it a few seconds, and then continue pinning the hem."

Rachel frowned. She didn't want to pin the hem in her dress. She wanted to go upstairs and finish reading her book. But she knew from the serious look on Mom's face that she'd better not mention it. She blew on her finger, but it didn't help much.

By the time Rachel finished pinning the hem, her finger felt a little better, but now she was bored. "Can't

I finish this tomorrow?" she asked Mom.

Mom shook her head. "You're almost done, Rachel. You just need to sew the hem in place."

Rachel threaded the needle and tied a knot. She was glad she wore glasses now and could see to do it. If she had tried threading a needle before she'd gotten glasses, she wouldn't have been able to see the tiny eye of the needle at all.

In and out. In and out. Rachel yawned as she made the tiniest stitches she could possibly make. This was so boring!

"Hannah's asleep now, Miriam," Grandpa said as he stopped rocking. "It's time for me to go to bed, too."

"Here, I'll go put her in her crib," Mom said. She rose from the sofa and took Hannah from Grandpa. "I'll be back in a few minutes, so keep sewing," she said to Rachel before she left the room.

Grandpa stood and yawned noisily. "*Gut nacht* [Good night], everyone."

"Why are you going to bed so early?" Rachel asked.

"I was busier than usual in my greenhouse today," he replied. "I'd counted on your help this afternoon, but since you had other things to do, I had to do everything on my own."

Rachel felt guilty for letting Grandpa down. She wished she'd been able to help him all afternoon instead of doing a bunch of chores she didn't enjoy.

"I'm sorry I couldn't help you, Grandpa. Maybe tomorrow I'll have more time."

Grandpa moved over to the sofa and squeezed Rachel's shoulder. "We'll have to see how it goes."

When Grandpa left the room, Rachel resumed her sewing. In and out. In and out. She wished she didn't have to make such little stitches. At this rate she'd be up all night trying to get the dress hemmed!

"That's it! The game's over, and I won!" Pap hollered.

Henry grunted and pushed back his chair. "It's your turn now, little *bruder* [brother]," he said, thumping Jacob's arm. "I hope you have better luck than I did. Pap's one tricky checkers player!"

"I can be pretty tricky, too." With a smug smile, Jacob dropped into Henry's chair. "Now we'll see who's the champion checkers player in this family!"

Pap rubbed his hands briskly together. "Jah, we'll see indeed!"

Rachel rolled her eyes. Jacob was such a braggart, and bragging was being prideful, which the bishop of their church had said wasn't a good thing. It would serve Jacob right to lose this game of checkers!

In and out. In and out. *Tick-tock. Tick-tock.* The clock on the mantel kept time with Rachel's stitches.

"King me, Pap!" Jacob shouted. "And then king me again!"

"Ach," Pap said with a grunt. "You outsmarted me

with that sneaky move, boy!"

Jacob chuckled. "I told you I was good at this game!"

Rachel rolled her eyes again and cut the end of her thread. Finally, she'd finished hemming her dress. She stuck the needle in the arm of the sofa, made a knot in the thread, and clipped it with the scissors. Then she wandered across the room to watch the checkers game. Pap had three kings, but Jacob had seven. Unless Pap improved, Jacob would probably win the game.

Rachel was tempted to offer Pap some suggestions but figured he wouldn't be too happy about that. Jacob didn't deserve to win—not when he thought he was so great at checkers.

Tick-tock. Tick-tock. Several minutes passed. Jacob managed to get two more kings. *Click! Click! Click!* He jumped Pap's last few checkers.

"I won!" Jacob pushed his chair back and waved his arms. "I'm the checkers champion in this house; that's for certain sure!"

Pap winked at Rachel. He probably thought Jacob was a big braggart, too.

"Whew, that game about wore me out!" Jacob shuffled across the room and flopped onto the sofa. "Yeow!" He leaped up and waved his hand in the air. "There's a giant *nodel* [needle] stuck in my hand!"

"Well, what's the matter with you, boy? Take the nodel out," Pap said.

Jacob hopped from one foot to the other. "I can't! It'll hurt!"

"Oh, don't be such a boppli. The nodel's not that big." Rachel hurried to Jacob and grabbed his hand. "If you hold real still, this won't hurt a bit." She grabbed the end of the needle and yanked. "There you go! Your hand's as good as new!"

Jacob's eyebrows furrowed as he scowled at Rachel. "You put that nodel in the sofa, didn't you?"

She nodded slowly. "I was going to take it out, but I forgot."

He shook his finger in her face. "I'll get even with you for this!" Before Rachel could respond, Jacob darted out of the room.

Rachel sank to the edge of the sofa and groaned.

Chapter 3
Getting Even

Rachel sat up with a start. She looked at the clock on the nightstand by her bed and realized she'd almost overslept. She scrambled out of bed and raced to her closet. Then she took off her nightgown, grabbed a dress from its hanger, and slipped it on. She picked up her sneakers and rushed to the dresser.

In a hurry to finish getting dressed, she jerked the bottom drawer of her dresser all the way out. *Crash!* It fell on the floor, spilling all her underclothes. She flopped down beside them and fumbled around until she found a pair of black stockings. In her hurry, she put both stockings on the same foot.

"Always trouble somewhere," she grumbled as she pulled the stockings off and started over again. This time she carefully put only one stocking on each foot.

Rachel stood and smoothed the wrinkles from her dress. Then she raced out of her room and down the stairs.

Rachel's stomach rumbled when she stepped into the kitchen and smelled bacon frying. "Mmm. . .I'm *hungerich* [hungry]," she said, rubbing her stomach. "How soon until breakfast is ready?"

"As soon as you go to the chicken coop and get more eggs." Mom motioned to the carton of eggs on the counter. "I only have four. That's not enough eggs for the six people living in this house."

"What about Jacob?" Rachel asked. "Can't he go to the chicken coop and check for eggs?'

Mom shook her head. "Jacob's helping Henry and Pap milk the cows and do outdoor chores."

Rachel frowned. She guessed she had no other choice than to do as Mom asked. She grabbed her jacket from the wall peg near the door and headed outside.

When she stepped onto the porch, a blustery breeze whipped through the trees and under the porch eaves. She shivered. "*Brr. . .*" Autumn had crept in while summer faded away. Soon winter would be here, and then she'd really be cold.

Rachel hurried to the chicken coop, opened the door, and stepped inside.

Crack! Crack! Crunch! Crunch!

Rachel looked down. Six eggs were lined up just inside the door, and she'd stepped on four of them! She clenched her fists until her fingers ached. "Jacob Yoder, you'll be sorry for this!"

She grabbed the two eggs that hadn't been broken

and checked each of the hens' nests. No more eggs. With a groan, she scurried out the door and raced back to the house.

Mom smiled when Rachel entered the kitchen. "Did you get some eggs?"

Rachel held out the two eggs. "Just these. The others were broken."

Mom frowned. "How'd they get broken?"

Rachel's face heated. "I—uh—stepped on them." She debated about telling Mom that she thought Jacob had put the eggs there on purpose, but decided against it. Mom might accuse her of being a tattletale. Or she might think Rachel had made up the story just to get Jacob in trouble.

"Well," Mom said with a sigh, "I guess we'll have to make do with the eggs we have this morning. We'll just have one apiece instead of two."

Rachel sighed in relief. At least Mom hadn't yelled at her for stepping on the eggs.

"Wash your hands and set the table, Rachel," Mom said, motioning to the silverware drawer.

Rachel glanced at the clock and hurried to do as she was told.

She'd just finished setting the table when Pap, Henry, Jacob, and Grandpa entered the kitchen.

"Mmm. . .bacon and eggs." Grandpa smacked his lips. "I could smell 'em as soon as I stepped out of my room."

"There's only one egg for each of us," Mom said, "but I've made plenty of bacon and toast, so I don't think anyone will go hungry."

Jacob gave Rachel a smug smile as he sat at the table, but then he quickly looked away.

Rachel ground her teeth together. *I just know he put those eggs by the chicken coop door!* she fumed. She remembered him saying last night that he would get even with her.

Rachel ate her toast and drank her juice, but nothing tasted right. She decided she'd get even with Jacob for getting even with her.

After breakfast, Jacob, Henry, and Pap went outside to do more chores, and Grandpa headed to his greenhouse.

"I need to feed the boppli now," Mom said, looking at Rachel and pushing her chair away from the table. "It may take me awhile, and I don't want you and Jacob to be late for school, so I'd like you to make yours and Jacob's lunches." Without waiting for Rachel to reply, Mom hurried from the room.

Rachel stomped to the refrigerator. She didn't mind making her own lunch, but she didn't see why she had to make Jacob's lunch, too. It wasn't fair! After what he'd done in the chicken coop, he should make her lunch this morning!

Rachel grabbed the handle of the refrigerator and yanked the door open. As she reached inside, she spotted a jar of peanut butter. Her hand stopped in midair when she spied a jar of brown mustard. *Hmm. . . I wonder. . .*

Rachel snatched the jar of mustard along with the jar of peanut butter and some of Mom's homemade strawberry jelly; then she shut the refrigerator door. She tromped back across the room and grabbed a loaf of bread from the pantry. Quickly, she made two sandwiches—one with peanut butter and jelly. But for the other sandwich, she mixed a hefty serving of brown mustard in the peanut butter. She put the normal peanut butter and jelly sandwich in her lunch pail and the other in Jacob's lunch pail.

"That should teach my bruder a good lesson," Rachel muttered. "He deserves it after making me step on those eggs!"

As Rachel walked along the path toward school, she glanced at Jacob and thought about the sandwich she'd made for his lunch. He'd sure be surprised when he bit into it at noon and discovered it was full of brown mustard with the peanut butter!

Swallowing back the feelings of guilt creeping into her heart, Rachel tried to concentrate on something else. She looked at the sun, which was trying to peek between the gray clouds. A flock of geese glided through the sky, and the trees lining the road swayed in the breeze. If Rachel didn't have so many troubling thoughts on her mind, she might have enjoyed this walk to school. Maybe she'd made a mistake in making Jacob that mustard sandwich.

When they entered the school yard, several children were playing in a pile of leaves. Rachel was tempted to join them, but the crisp autumn air made her shiver, so she hurried inside.

All morning Rachel had a hard time concentrating on her studies. She kept thinking about the sandwich waiting for Jacob in his lunch pail.

Maybe I could sneak it out of there before it's time for lunch, Rachel thought. *But then when Jacob goes to eat his lunch, he'll wonder why he has no sandwich.*

Rachel nibbled the tip of her fingernail as she continued to mull things over. By the time Teacher Elizabeth dismissed the class to get their lunches, Rachel had bitten almost every one of her nails.

I need to quit worrying about this, she finally decided. *Jacob deserves that mustard sandwich. Jah, he surely does!*

"Say, Rachel, what happened to all of your fingernails? They look really short," Orlie said as he opened his lunch pail and sat on the back porch.

"They're in her stomach," Jacob said before Rachel could reply. "She's supposed to quit that bad habit of chewing on her nails, but she's still a little boppli, so she probably won't."

Rachel's face heated. "You're a mean bruder, Jacob,"

she mumbled. He really did deserve that mustard sandwich!

Jacob snickered and plopped down beside Orlie. "I'm not mean, but I'm sure hungerich!"

He opened his lunch pail and removed his sandwich. Then he unwrapped it and took a big bite. His eyes widened, his lips puckered, and he coughed as he spit the piece of sandwich out onto the porch. "Ugh! What's wrong with my peanut butter and jelly sandwich?"

Rachel clamped her lips shut and looked away.

Jacob took a drink of milk from his thermos. Then he pushed Rachel's arm. "You made my sandwich with mustard, didn't you?"

She nodded slowly and turned to face him. "I did it to get even with you for setting those eggs in front of the chicken coop door so I'd step on them."

Jacob scowled. "What you did to me was ten times worse than what I did to you! You should have tasted that sandwich, Rachel. It was *baremlich* [terrible]!" He nudged Rachel's arm again. "Mom's not gonna like it when I tell her what you did."

Rachel glared at him. "You do and I'll tell her about the eggs."

Ping! Ping! Ping! Rain started splattering on the roof and blew under the eaves of the porch. All the scholars who'd been sitting there grabbed their lunch pails and ran into the schoolhouse.

Rachel hopped up, but Jacob just sat there, staring at his sandwich.

"Aren't you coming inside?" Rachel asked.

He glared up at her. "Give me your sandwich!"

"What?"

"I said, 'Give me your sandwich!' "

She shook her head. "Why should I?"

"Because you ruined mine!"

"You ruined all the eggs we should have had for breakfast."

"Did not." Jacob tossed the rest of his sandwich into his lunch pail. "You ruined the eggs when you stepped on them."

"I wouldn't have stepped on them if you hadn't put them on the floor by the door."

Jacob folded his arms and glared at her.

"Well, I don't know about you, but I'm not going to stay out here and get wet." Rachel hurried into the schoolhouse and shut the door.

As Jacob and Rachel walked home from school that afternoon, Rachel walked slower than she normally would have. The rain had stopped, but mud puddles filled the path by the road. She tried to dodge them, but one was so big she stepped right in, soaking her sneakers and splattering the hem of her dress. Her wet shoes made a squeaking sound as she continued to walk, and when she came to the next puddle, she jumped right over it.

Rachel usually liked coming home from school, but not today. Besides the extra chores she knew would be waiting, she was afraid Jacob would tell Mom about the mustard she'd put on his sandwich. Then she'd be in big trouble with Mom. Well, if he did tell, then she'd tell on him, too!

As Rachel turned into their driveway, Jacob ran past her and made a beeline for the house. Rachel ran as fast as she could, but Jacob leaped onto the porch ahead of her. Rachel's face was hot, and she was out of breath when she entered the house.

"Please don't tell Mom about the sandwich," she whispered, tapping Jacob on the shoulder.

"What was that?"

"I said, 'Please don't tell Mom about the sandwich,'" she said a little louder.

"Huh?"

She poked his arm. "You should get your hearing tested!"

"You don't have to yell. I'm standing right beside you, little bensel."

"Don't call me that!"

Jacob snickered.

When they entered the kitchen, Rachel saw a note on the table from Mom. Mom had gone to Esther's to see how she was doing.

Rachel plopped down on the floor and removed

her wet sneakers. After being out in the chilly, damp weather, Rachel thought the kitchen felt warm and cozy. The longer she sat there waiting for Mom to get home, the more nervous she became.

I sure wish I hadn't made that mustard sandwich. I sure hope Jacob keeps quiet about it, she thought.

When Mom stepped into the kitchen a short time later, Jacob rushed to her and said, "You know that sandwich Rachel made for me this morning?"

Mom nodded. "What about the sandwich?"

"She put brown mustard on it!" Jacob wrinkled his nose and made a horrible face. "It tasted baremlich, Mom!"

Mom turned to Rachel and frowned. "What in all the world possessed you to do something so mean?"

"I—I did it to get even with Jacob for putting eggs on the floor of the chicken coop this morning so I'd step on them," Rachel said.

Mom peered at Jacob over the top of her glasses. "Is that true, son?"

He nodded and hung his head.

"You two should be ashamed of yourselves. Don't you remember what the Bible says about doing unto others as you would like them to do to you? We're supposed to love everyone, even our enemies. We're not supposed to do mean things or try to get even with anyone." Mom pointed to Jacob. "For the next week it will be your job to clean the chicken coop and gather eggs every day." She pointed to Rachel. "It will be your job to make Jacob's lunch every day, and you have to fix him something he likes."

Jacob grunted. Rachel gasped. So this was what she got for trying to get even!

Chapter 4

Daydreaming

"I shouldn't have to do this," Rachel complained to Jacob as she began making his lunch the following morning.

"Then you shouldn't have fixed that mustard sandwich for me yesterday." Jacob peered over Rachel's shoulder. "You'd better put all the things I like in my lunch pail today. Mom said you have to."

"Stop hovering!" Rachel shooed him away with her hand. "And for your information, Mom didn't say I had to fix *everything* that you like. She said I have to fix *something* you like."

Jacob put his fingers around his throat and made a gagging sound. "Well, I don't like mustard sandwiches, so you'd better not make that again!"

"Don't worry, I won't." Rachel frowned at him. "And you'd better not put eggs on the chicken floor ever again!"

He grunted. "Why would I, when I'm the one

going to the chicken coop to fetch eggs every morning? I wouldn't want to step on any of those eggs; that's for sure."

Rachel slathered a bunch of tuna on Jacob's sandwich and held her nose. Tuna was one of his favorite sandwiches, but she didn't like the strong smell. It wasn't something she cared to eat, either.

"What are you putting in my lunch for dessert?" Jacob asked, leaning on the counter with both arms.

"I thought I'd put in an orange."

Jacob wrinkled his nose. "I don't want an orange. I want something else."

"How about an apple or a banana?" Rachel asked.

He shook his head.

"What do you want?"

"I'd like two powdered sugar doughnuts." Jacob held up three fingers. "On second thought, make it three—no, I think four."

Rachel rolled her eyes. "You're such a *sau* [pig]. *Oink! Oink!*"

"I'm not a pig. I just know I'll be hungry by lunchtime." Jacob smacked his lips and patted his stomach. "Some powdered sugar doughnuts sound real good to me."

"Is a tuna sandwich and four powdered sugar doughnuts all that you want?" Rachel asked as she reached for the container of doughnuts.

Jacob tapped his chin a couple of times. "Let's see

now. . . . How about a thermos full of chocolate milk? Oh, and I'd also like some potato chips and a piece of leftover chicken."

"*Oink! Oink! Oink!*"

Jacob poked Rachel's arm. "Stop saying that. I'm not a sau!"

"Jah, you are. Only a pig eats that much at one time."

Jacob stood straight and tall. "I eat a lot because, in case you hadn't noticed, I'm growing into a man."

"*Puh!*" Rachel flapped her hand at him. "You're not a man. You're an *oink-oink* sau!"

"Am not!"

"Are so!"

"Am not!"

"What's all the yelling about?" Grandpa asked when he stepped into the room. "I could hear you two clear down the hall."

"She's calling me names."

"He's acting like a sau."

Grandpa motioned to Rachel. "Would you please explain to me what's going on?"

She pointed to Jacob's lunch pail. "Just because I'm supposed to make his lunch, he expects me to fix a whole bunch of food that he doesn't even need. So I called him a sau."

Grandpa frowned. "Jacob's wrong if he expects you to fix more food than he needs, but that doesn't give you an excuse to call him names." He put his thumb under Rachel's chin. "I think you should apologize to your bruder, don't you?"

Rachel stared at the floor. "I don't see why I have to apologize. He's the one who started it by asking for so much food."

"Well, if she hadn't been grumbling about having to fix my lunch, I wouldn't have asked for more food." Jacob glared at Rachel. "*Die Rachel is die ganz zeit am grummle* [Rachel is grumbling all the time]."

"I am not!" Rachel shouted.

"Are too!"

"Am—"

Grandpa held up both hands. "That's enough! I want you both to apologize for the things you've said to each other, and you'd better be quick about it."

"Sorry," Jacob and Rachel mumbled at the same time.

Grandpa motioned to Jacob's lunch pail. "Now finish the lunches, Rachel, or you'll both be late for school."

"I'm almost done with Jacob's lunch," Rachel said. "And then I'll need to fix my own."

Grandpa nodded at Jacob. "Why don't you wait outside for Rachel? She'll be along in a few minutes."

"Okay." Jacob slipped into his jacket, plunked his hat on his head, and hurried out the door, letting it slam shut with a bang.

Rachel sighed. "He makes me so angry! Sometimes

I wish I didn't have any *brieder* [brothers]."

Grandpa patted Rachel's arm. "I'm sure all sisters feel that way at times. Brothers sometimes wish they didn't have any sisters, too. I know I felt that way when I was a *buwe* [boy]." He gently squeezed Rachel's arm. "Remember that even though Jacob sometimes gives you a hard time, he's still a member of this family, and I'm sure he loves you. Just try to be nice to him, Rachel."

Rachel nodded slowly. "I love him, too. I just wish he'd be nice to me all of the time."

"Maybe someday he will—when you're both grown up."

Rachel grunted. "Jah, if that ever happens."

As Rachel and Jacob walked to school, Rachel kicked at the stones along the path while she watched the falling leaves drift on the wind. It was easier than talking to Jacob, and a lot more fun.

"What are you looking at, Rachel?" Jacob asked, poking her in the back.

"I'm looking at the autumn leaves and thinking how much fun it would be if I could fly through the air like a leaf or a bird."

Jacob grunted. "What a daydreamer you are. Won't you ever grow up?"

"Grown-ups sometimes daydream," Rachel said. "Grandpa does it whenever he stands on his head. He told me so once."

Jacob shook his head. "That's not why Grandpa stands on his head, and you know it. He stands on his head so he can think better."

Rachel kicked another pebble with the toe of her sneaker. "A lot you know, Jacob Yoder."

"I know more than you think, and I don't daydream or grumble all the time."

As they entered the school yard, Jacob ran off. He bounded up to Orlie Troyer and shouted, "Guess what, Orlie? My little sister's a daydreamer!"

Orlie snickered and looked at Rachel.

Rachel gritted her teeth. If she hadn't been trying so hard to do as Grandpa suggested, she'd have said something mean to Jacob.

Rachel glanced around the school yard, hoping to find her friend Audra, but she wasn't anywhere in sight. A few minutes later, the school bell rang, and Rachel followed the other scholars inside. She was disappointed to see that Audra wasn't at her desk. She wondered if Audra might be sick.

Ding! Ding! Teacher Elizabeth rang the bell on her desk. Just then, Audra and her brother Brian raced into the room with red faces and breathing heavily.

"Sorry we're late," Audra said, looking at Elizabeth. "Our mamm's sick in bed with the flu, so we had extra chores to do this morning."

"It's all right; you're not that late," Elizabeth said.

"Just take your seats."

A few minutes later, the scholars rose to their feet and recited the Lord's Prayer. As the children sang a few songs, Rachel gazed out the window at some birds sitting on the branch of a maple tree. She wished she could be outside to hear the birds sing.

"Singing's over, and it's time to take your seat," Audra whispered in Rachel's ear.

Rachel's face warmed and she hurried to her desk.

As Elizabeth handed out the arithmetic assignment, Rachel's mind began to wander. *I wonder what Grandpa's doing right now. I wish I could be there helping in the greenhouse. It would be a lot more fun than being cooped up in the schoolhouse all day.*

"Rachel, are you working on your arithmetic assignment?"

Rachel jerked up straight when she heard her teacher's voice. "Uh—yes, I'm almost done." She looked down at her paper and realized that she'd only done two of the twelve problems.

Tap! Tap! Tap! Rachel tapped the edge of her pencil on the side of her desk. *I wonder what Mary's doing right now. Is she doing arithmetic at her school in Indiana? Does Mary like school this year, or does she wish she could be at home, too?*

Rachel glanced out the window again. She wished it was open so she could hear the birds singing and smell the fresh fall air. She wished she could gather some fallen leaves and compare their sizes, shapes, and colors.

"All right, class. Your time is up," Elizabeth said. "Please pass your papers to the front of the room."

Rachel gulped. Her paper wasn't done. She couldn't turn it in with only two problems solved. She'd get a bad grade for sure.

Orlie, who sat in front of Rachel, turned around. "Where's your paper, Rachel? You're supposed to turn it in now."

Rachel moistened her lips with the tip of her tongue. "I—uh—"

"You'd better give it to me, Rachel," Orlie said.

With a sigh, Rachel handed her paper over to Orlie, along with the ones from the children behind her. Orlie stood and walked up to Elizabeth's desk; then he handed her the papers.

When he returned to his desk, he glanced at Rachel. "Have you been daydreaming again?" he whispered.

She just looked away.

When it was time for morning recess, Rachel jumped out of her chair and raced for the back door. She could hardly wait to get outside!

"Rachel Yoder, can I see you a minute, please?"

Rachel whirled around. "What is it?" she asked her teacher.

Elizabeth motioned for Rachel to come to her

desk. Then she held up Rachel's arithmetic paper. "Why isn't this done, Rachel? You had plenty of time to do the assignment, and it wasn't that difficult."

Rachel shifted from one foot to the other. "Well, I—uh—got distracted when I was looking out the window, and—"

"You were daydreaming instead of doing your schoolwork?" Elizabeth leaned across the desk and stared hard at Rachel.

Rachel nodded slowly as her face grew warm.

Elizabeth handed Rachel's unfinished paper to her. "I want you to sit at your desk and finish this assignment right now."

"But—but what about recess?"

Elizabeth shook her head. "No recess for you this morning. You must learn to be more responsible and to do your assignment like the other scholars did." She squinted her eyes at Rachel. "There's a time and a place for daydreaming, but it's not here at school. Do you understand?"

Rachel nodded and swallowed around the lump in her throat. She didn't like missing recess, and she didn't like being scolded by her teacher!

When it was time for lunch, Rachel grabbed her lunch pail and hurried outside to eat on the porch with several other scholars, including Jacob.

Rachel ate her peanut butter and jelly sandwich

first; then she took out the doughnut she'd put in her lunch pail. When she bit into the doughnut, powdered sugar poofed out, sprinkling the front of her dress. She laughed and popped the last piece into her mouth. Then she licked her fingers.

"Grow up, Rachel," Jacob said. "Only a boppli licks her fingers."

"That's not true," Rachel said. "I've seen you lick your fingers when Mom serves fried chicken. I think everyone in our family does."

Jacob shrugged. "Maybe so, but you lick yours more than anyone else. Besides that, you're a boppli who likes to daydream and grumble all the time." Jacob gulped down the last of his doughnuts, took a drink of chocolate milk, and wiped his mouth with the back of his hand.

"I do not daydream or grumble all the time! You're just a—" The scripture verse Grandpa had mentioned the other day popped into Rachel's head. She clamped her mouth shut.

"I'm a what?" Jacob asked, nudging Rachel's arm.

"Nothing," she mumbled.

"So I'm a nothing, huh?"

"I didn't mean that. I just meant—oh, never mind!" Rachel grabbed her lunch pail and scooted to the other end of the porch. She decided it was best not to talk to Jacob at all.

When Rachel arrived home from school that

afternoon, she smelled the spicy aroma of hot apple cider as soon as she entered the kitchen. *Yum!* She licked her lips in anticipation.

Mom stood at the stove, stirring the cider in a big kettle. She turned and smiled at Rachel. "Did you have a *gut* [good] day?"

"It was okay." Rachel chose not to mention that she'd missed morning recess to finish her arithmetic assignment. She also didn't mention the trouble she'd had with Jacob when she'd made his lunch.

"Where's Jacob?" Mom asked.

"He went to the chicken coop. Said he wanted to clean it first thing so he'd have some free time to do something fun." Rachel's stomach rumbled. "I'm hungerich," she said, sitting at the table. "Are there any more of those powdered sugar doughnuts?"

Mom shook her head. "I gave the last two to Henry and your *daed* [dad] after lunch." Her forehead wrinkled. "I thought there were a lot more when I put them away last night. Did you put some in your lunch pails this morning?"

Rachel nodded. "Jacob insisted on having four, and I had one."

"Oh, I see," Mom said.

"So is there anything for me to eat?" Rachel asked.

Mom motioned to the refrigerator. "You can have some cheese if you like."

"Just cheese?"

"How about some crackers to go with it?"

"Jah, okay." Rachel figured cheese and crackers would be better than nothing, so she headed to the pantry to get the box of crackers.

By the time Rachel had fixed a plate of cheese and crackers, the apple cider was heated.

"Here you go," Mom said, placing a mug in front of Rachel.

A curl of steam drifted up from the cider, and Rachel sniffed deeply. "Mmm. . .this smells *appenditlich* [delicious]. *Danki* [Thanks], Mom."

"You're welcome." Mom poured herself a cup of cider and was about to sit down when—*Waaa! Waaa!*—Hannah's shrill cry floated into the room.

"Guess I'd better tend to your baby sister." Mom set her cup on the counter and hurried from the room.

Rachel ate her cheese and crackers and had just finished her cider when Mom called from the other room, "Rachel, your daed and Henry are in the barn grooming the horses. Would you please run out there and ask if they'd like some cider?"

"Okay, Mom." Rachel set her dishes in the sink and scurried out the door.

She'd just stepped off the porch when she spotted Snowball playing with a ball of string.

"Here, kitty, kitty!" Rachel called, clapping her hands.

Snowball's ears twitched, and she took off for the

barn. Rachel raced after her.

When Rachel entered the barn, she didn't see any sign of Snowball. Cuddles wasn't anywhere in sight, either.

Rachel flopped onto a bale of hay, leaned her head against the wall, and closed her eyes. Soon she was daydreaming about going on a wild amusement park ride, like the one she'd gone on when she went to Hershey Park with Sherry and Dave this summer.

Rachel felt something tickle her nose, and her eyelids fluttered open. Jacob stood over her with a goose feather in his hand.

"*Absatz* [Stop]!" Rachel pushed his hand away. "Leave me alone!"

"What's the matter, little bensel? Are you upset because I woke you, or were you daydreaming again?"

"Stop saying that to me!" she shouted so loudly that Snowball ran out from behind a bale of hay with her ears straight back. She hissed loudly as she raced out of the barn.

"Now look what you've done!" Jacob tickled Rachel under the chin with the feather. "You scared that poor cat of yours right out of her fur!"

"Did not!"

"Did so!"

Rachel put her hand over her mouth to keep from screaming. She was trying to be nice to Jacob, but he was sure making it hard.

"Daydreamer, daydreamer," Jacob taunted as he continued to tickle her with the feather.

Rachel jumped up and shook her finger in his face. "Absatz, right now!"

"What's all the ruckus about in here?" Pap asked, stepping out of one of the horse's stalls.

Rachel pointed to Jacob. "Ask him; he started it."

Pap turned to face Jacob. "What's the problem?"

"There's no problem, Pap." Jacob gave Rachel an innocent-looking grin. "I was just tickling her with a goose feather and she got upset."

"He was doing more than that," Rachel said. "He was picking on me because I like to daydream."

Pap shook Jacob's shoulder. "Stop picking on your sister and find something else to do with your time."

Jacob scuffed the toe of his boot against the concrete floor. "Guess I'll go to the house and see if Mom made me a snack."

Just then Rachel remembered the reason Mom had sent her to the barn. "I almost forgot," she said to Pap. "Mom wanted me to ask if you and Henry would like some hot apple cider."

Pap nodded. "That sounds good. Run back to the house and tell her we'll be in as soon as we finish grooming the horses." He squeezed Rachel's arm. "And no daydreaming along the way."

As Rachel left the barn, she said to herself, "What's wrong with a little daydreaming now and then? I'm just doing a bit of wishful thinking."

Chapter 5

Borrowing Brings Sorrowing

For the next several days, Rachel tried not to daydream so much. She wanted people to think she was growing up. So instead of daydreaming, she kept busy doing her homework and chores and helping Grandpa in the greenhouse.

On Saturday morning, Rachel headed for the greenhouse, hoping she could spend most of the day there.

"Where are you, Grandpa?" she called when she stepped inside and didn't see him working with any of the flowers.

"I'm back here in my office." Grandpa's voice sounded muffled, like he was talking underwater.

I'll bet Grandpa's standing on his head again, Rachel thought.

She hurried to his office, and sure enough, Grandpa was in one corner of the room, with his feet in the air and his hands resting on the floor.

"Are you trying to clear your head?" Rachel asked, bending down so she could see Grandpa's face.

He gave her an upside-down smile. "Jah, that's what I'm doing all right."

"Should I wait until you're done, or is there something I could be doing in the greenhouse right now?" Rachel asked.

"Once my head's clear enough, we'll prune some of the plants," Grandpa said. "In the meantime, why don't you check the Christmas cacti I recently got in and see if they need any water?"

"Sure, I can do that." Rachel skipped out of the room and over to the shelf where Grandpa had put the plants. She was about to put her finger in the dirt to see if the first one was dry when she remembered that Grandpa had recently bought a little gauge that showed whether or not the plant needed water.

She found the gauge in the drawer under one of the workbenches and stuck it in the dirt of the first cactus. When she saw the moisture reading, she smiled. The plant still had plenty of water. Down the row she went, testing each cactus with the gauge. Only one plant needed water, and she took care of that right away.

When Rachel put the gauge away, she spotted a book about wildflowers on the shelf. It looked interesting, so she picked it up, took a seat on a wooden stool, and opened the book to the table of contents. The first section included a description of several kinds of wildflowers. The next section told some places where wildflowers might grow. There was even a section about pressing wildflowers and putting them in an album, or using them to make bookmarks, postcards, and stationery.

Rachel hummed as she studied a page showing hooded cluster plants such as jack-in-the-pulpit, sweet flag, and yellow skunk cabbage.

"What are you reading?" Grandpa asked when he entered the room.

Rachel held up the book. "It's called *Wildflowers*, and it looks like an interesting book. I've never seen it here before. Is it new, Grandpa?"

He nodded. "I thought it might be fun to grow some wildflowers in the garden next spring. What do you think of that idea?"

"I think it's a very good idea." Rachel smiled and pointed to the page she had opened. "I'd like to study this book some more and learn about pressing flowers so I can make some pretty cards and things. Can I borrow the book for a few days?"

Grandpa tugged his beard and frowned in thought as his bushy gray eyebrows pulled together so they almost met above the bridge of his nose. "Well, let's see now. . . ." He gave his beard one more quick pull. "I guess it would be all right, but I want you to remember one thing."

"What's that, Grandpa?" Rachel sat up straighter and listened with both ears. She remembered the things that were really important to her—at least most of the time.

"I'd be happy to loan you the book, but I need to know that you'll take good care of it, and I'd like to have it back by the end of next week."

"I promise I'll take care of the book, and I'll be sure to return it to you next week," Rachel said with a nod.

After lunch that afternoon, Grandpa said he wouldn't need Rachel's help in the greenhouse for the rest of the day. Rachel decided it would be a good time to read some more from the wildflower book.

She carried the book outside to the porch, sat on the porch swing, and opened the book to the section that told about pressing flowers. She'd only read a few pages when Mom stepped outside and said, "Jacob's having an ice cream cone. Would you like one, Rachel?"

Rachel nodded eagerly. She loved ice cream, especially strawberry-flavored ice cream, which Pap had made last night after supper.

"Would you like to come into the kitchen, or would you rather eat your cone out here?" Mom asked.

"I'd rather eat it out here."

"Okay, I'll bring the cone right out." Mom went into the house and returned to the porch a few minutes later with a sugar cone heaped high with strawberry ice cream.

"You'd better set that book aside while you're eating this," Mom said, handing Rachel the cone. "Grandpa wouldn't like it if you got ice cream on any of the pages."

"Okay, Mom." Rachel set the book on the small table nearby. "Oh, by the way, I was wondering what time Esther and Rudy will be coming over for the bonfire tonight."

Mom shook her head. "When I checked the answering machine in the phone shed earlier, there was a message from Rudy. He said they wouldn't be coming because Esther isn't feeling up to it."

"That's too bad. Will Pap build a bonfire anyway?"

"I don't think so, Rachel. I believe we'll have to do it some other time."

Rachel was disappointed, but before she could say so, Mom went back in the house.

Rachel sighed and stared at her ice cream cone, wondering which side to lick first. She was glad it was a warm, sunny day. Before long it would be too cold to eat ice cream outside. She was also glad that Jacob had chosen to stay inside. She didn't need him out here pestering her. Knowing Jacob, he'd probably eat his cone really fast, and then he'd expect her to give him a couple of licks from hers.

She crinkled her nose. No way would she let Jacob

get any of his germs on her ice cream cone!

Slurp! Slurp! Rachel licked one side and then the other. "Yum! This is appenditlich," she said, smacking her lips. When she'd eaten half the cone, she reached for the wildflower book.

She placed the book in her lap and opened it to the page that showed how to make a bookmark using dried flowers and leaves. It would be fun to create a pretty bookmark and send it to Mary in her next letter. Maybe Rachel would even make some stationery using dried flowers.

Rachel lifted her ice cream cone to take another bite, when—*floop!*—Snowball leaped from the porch railing and bumped Rachel's arm, knocking the cone out of her hand.

Rachel gasped when a blob of ice cream landed on the book, right in the middle of a picture of a hollyhock plant!

"Ach, Snowball, look what you've done to Grandpa's *buch* [book]!" Rachel pushed the kitten away and jumped up. She had to do something quickly or the book might be ruined.

She raced into the house, grabbed a sponge from the kitchen sink, turned on the water, and soaked the sponge. Then she squeezed the excess water from the sponge and raced back outside.

"No, no, no!" she hollered when she spotted Snowball sitting on the swing, licking the ice cream that had fallen onto the book. "Get away from there, you silly *bussli* [kitten]!" She pushed Snowball aside and picked up the book. There wasn't much ice cream left on the page, but now there was a big ugly-looking pink stain where the ice cream had been.

Rachel's heart pounded, and her head began to throb. "I can't give the book back to Grandpa like this," she whimpered. "If I do, he'll say I didn't take good care of it."

She sat on the edge of the swing feeling sorry for herself. Why did she always have so much trouble? She hated feeling helpless like this.

After several minutes, an idea popped into Rachel's head. *I'll hide the book. Maybe Grandpa will forget he loaned it to me and I won't have to tell him what happened.*

Rachel jumped off the swing and raced for the barn. She would hide the book in the hayloft where no one would see.

The next several days went by, but Grandpa didn't mention the book. With each day, Rachel felt guiltier and guiltier for not telling Grandpa what she'd done with his book. Finally, when she could stand it no more, she decided to go to the hayloft and get the book.

Rachel entered the barn and looked around to be sure no one was watching. Then she climbed the ladder to the hayloft and hurried to the mound of hay where she'd hidden the book. She reached inside and felt all around. The book was gone!

"No! No! No!" Rachel hollered. "This can't be happening!"

Rachel remembered the time she'd put her glasses inside a box and hidden it in the hayloft. Jacob had found them and hidden them in his room to teach Rachel a lesson. He'd obviously done it to her again.

Rachel sprinted down the ladder and ran all the way to house. She found Jacob in his room, sprawled on his bed, reading a book.

"Give it to me!" she demanded.

"Give what to you?" Jacob mumbled without looking at her.

"The wildflower book."

Jacob set his book aside and sat up. "I have no idea what you're talking about. This book is about a dog."

Rachel gritted her teeth. "Don't act so innocent. You went into the hayloft and took the book I hid there."

Jacob's raised his eyebrows. "You hid a book there?"

She nodded slowly. "Please give it back."

Jacob lifted the book he held. "This is the only book I know anything about, and it has nothing to do with wildflowers."

"I know you took that book!" Rachel shouted. "*Ferwas bischt allfat so schtarkeppich* [Why are you always so stubborn]?"

"I'm not being stubborn. I'm telling you the truth."

Rachel moved closer to his bed and peered at the book. It was about a dog. "So you never saw the book about wildflowers?"

"Nope."

She scratched her head. "Then what could have happened to it?"

Jacob shrugged his shoulders. "Beats me." He motioned to the door. "Now go away and leave me in peace to read my book."

Rachel shuffled out the door, feeling hopeless and sad. What if she never found Grandpa's book? How could she explain that to him?

Rachel could hardly eat supper that night, and when she went to bed she couldn't sleep. She could only think about the missing book and how she wished she'd never borrowed it in the first place.

When she got up the next morning, she knew she needed to tell Grandpa the truth.

Rachel waited until after breakfast. Since it was Saturday and there was no school, she knew Grandpa would expect her to help him in the greenhouse.

She'd just started for the greenhouse when she spotted Grandma Yoder's horse and buggy coming up their driveway.

"*Guder mariye* [Good morning], Rachel," Grandma said after she'd stopped the buggy. "I've come to do some baking with your mamm. Are you going to join us?"

Rachel shook her head. "I'm going to the greenhouse to help Grandpa." She kicked at a pebble with the toe of her sneaker and stared at the ground.

"You seem to be *umgerennt* [upset]. Is something wrong?" Grandma asked.

Rachel nodded and lifted her gaze to meet Grandma's. "I–I've lost something important and can't find it." She sniffed a couple of times. "I think my name should be Trouble, because trouble seems to find me wherever I go." *Borrowing brings sorrowing,* she thought. *At least it has for me.*

Grandma smiled at Rachel. "Remember now, no matter how much trouble you have, it too will pass."

"I'll try to remember," Rachel mumbled. As she headed for the greenhouse, a sudden breeze rattled the leaves on the trees. She shivered and pulled the collar of her jacket tighter around her neck.

When Rachel entered the greenhouse a few minutes later, she found Grandpa in his office, sitting at his desk.

"I—I have something I need to tell you," she said tearfully.

"What is it, Rachel?" Grandpa asked.

"I spilled ice cream on the wildflower book I borrowed from you, and—and then I hid it, but now it's missing."

"Ah, I see." Grandpa reached into his desk drawer

and pulled out a book. It was the wildflower book. "Is this what you've been looking for?"

Rachel was so surprised she could hardly talk.

"I found this book in the hayloft when I went there looking for a box." Grandpa frowned. "What do you have to say about this, Rachel?"

Rachel hung her head, unable to meet Grandpa's gaze. "I—I'm sorry. I shouldn't have been looking at the book while I was eating ice cream." *Sniff. Sniff.* "And I shouldn't have hid the book in the hayloft to keep you from finding out what I'd done." Tears streamed down her cheeks. "I'll save up my money and buy you a new book."

Grandpa shook his head. "That's not necessary. The book isn't ruined; just one page has a stain on it." He leaned forward with his elbows on the desk. "I do want you to learn a lesson from this, however."

Rachel's heart hammered in her chest as she waited to hear what her punishment would be. Would Grandpa tell Mom and Pap? Would they give her a *bletsching* [spanking] or make her do a bunch more chores? "I'm really sorry, and I know I deserve to be punished," she said, nearly choking on a sob.

Grandpa pulled Rachel into his arms. "It's good that you've apologized to me, but you need to tell God you're sorry, too." He patted her back. "A sign that a person is growing up is when that person is willing to admit to doing something wrong, and to make it right with the person involved and also with God."

Rachel nodded and bowed her head. She'd make things right with God right now. And the next time she asked to borrow anything, she would try extra hard to make sure accidents didn't happen!

Chapter 6

Mistakes

"Rachel, don't forget to put your sheets and clothes in the laundry basket before you leave for school," Mom called up the stairs on Monday morning. "And hurry; we're ready to eat breakfast!"

Rachel cupped her hands around her mouth and hollered, "Okay, Mom!"

She dashed across the room, opened her closet door, and stepped inside to get her dirty clothes. She looked around and noticed her jump rope lying on the shelf. She scooped it up.

I'll take this to school today and play with it at recess, she decided.

"Rachel, are you coming?" Mom called again.

"Jah, I'll be there soon."

Rachel noticed the stack of newspapers she'd placed on top of the flowers Grandpa had given her to press several days ago.

"I'd better check and see how they're doing,"

Rachel said, kneeling. She lifted the newspapers and the cardboard covering the flowers. They looked pretty good. Soon they'd be ready to use in a bookmark or a card. Rachel could hardly wait! She sat several minutes, thinking about all the different designs she could make.

Rachel's stomach rumbled and she remembered that she was hungry. So she left the closet, hurried out of her room, and skipped down the stairs.

When Rachel entered the kitchen, she found Mom clearing dishes off the table. Grandpa sat by the fireplace reading a newspaper, but Rachel saw no sign of Jacob, Henry, or Pap.

"*Hoscht du schunn geese* [Have you already eaten]?" Rachel asked, stepping up to Mom.

Mom nodded and placed the bowls and cups into the sink.

Rachel's mouth dropped open like a broken window hinge. "You ate breakfast without me?"

"That's right," said Mom. "I called you several times, but you didn't come, so we ate without you."

Rachel's stomach rumbled as she stared at the table. "Can I have some breakfast now?"

Mom shook her head and motioned to the clock on the wall. "I'm afraid there's no time for that, Rachel. You still have to feed the chickens and check for eggs. Then you'll need to head to school." Mom's forehead wrinkled. "You should have come when I called you for breakfast."

Rachel stood frozen, unable to say a word. She could hardly believe Mom would send her to school without any breakfast. She bit her bottom lip to keep from crying, and then she looked at Grandpa, hoping he'd come to her rescue.

"Rachel, you've developed a bad habit of fooling around and not doing what you're told," he said. "Bad habits are like a comfortable bed: They're easy to get into but hard to get out of."

Rachel swallowed around the lump in her throat as she gave a quick nod. Then she grabbed her jacket from the wall peg and rushed out the back door. Maybe if she fed the chickens quickly, Mom would let her have some breakfast.

The shrill cry of a crow drew Rachel's gaze upward, but she had no time to dawdle. She dashed across the yard to the chicken coop and jerked open the door.

Quickly, she scooped out the chicken feed and poured some into the feeders. The chickens appeared to have plenty of water, so she decided not to add any more. She glanced in each of the nesting boxes but didn't see any eggs.

"The hurrier I go, the behinder I get," Rachel said as she raced out the door.

"I'm done feeding the chickens," Rachel said when she returned to the kitchen. "Can I have some breakfast now?"

Mom handed Rachel an apple. "There's no time

for that. Jacob's already left for school, and even if you leave right now, you'll probably be late."

Rachel's forehead wrinkled. "Jacob left without me?"

Mom nodded. "I didn't think it would be fair to make him wait for you and then have both of you late for school. I told him to go on without you."

Rachel looked at Grandpa. "Will you give me a ride to school so I won't be late?"

He shook his head. "Sorry, Rachel. Not this time. I have a customer coming to pick up some plants in a few minutes. I need to get out to my greenhouse right now."

Rachel looked at Mom. "Can't Pap or Henry take me to school?"

"No," Mom said. "They left to run some errands in town right after breakfast."

"Could you take me, then?"

"Sorry, Rachel, but I have washing to do and can't leave the baby." Mom handed Rachel her backpack and lunch pail. "Hurry to school now."

"B—but you always say I shouldn't walk to school alone," Rachel stammered.

"I think you're old enough now. Besides, you have no other choice." Mom shooed Rachel toward the door. "Schnell!"

Rachel headed up the path toward school. The leaves on the ground curled up on the edges as the breeze whistled them along. Rachel's feet dragged with each step she took. Besides knowing she was going to be late, she was tired from staying up past her bedtime last night. She decided she might as well take her time getting to school.

"Guess that's what I get for reading when I should have been sleeping, and for not paying attention when Mom called me to breakfast," she mumbled, feeling sorry for herself. "It's not fair that everyone ate breakfast without me. Someone should have come upstairs and told me it was time to eat."

By the time Rachel got to school, she felt even worse. When Rachel entered the schoolhouse, Elizabeth stood at the blackboard, writing the arithmetic assignment, so Rachel knew she'd missed the morning prayer and the songs they always sang.

As Rachel stepped down the aisle toward her desk, Elizabeth turned and frowned at her. "You're late, Rachel."

Rachel nodded. "Jah, I know. I woke up late, and then I—"

Elizabeth motioned to Rachel's desk. "Please take your seat and get out your arithmetic book. We can talk about your reason for being late during recess."

Rachel swallowed hard as her throat started to burn. She knew she probably wouldn't be allowed to go outside and play during recess. Elizabeth would probably have some work for Rachel to do during recess. She might even have to stay after school because of her tardiness.

Rachel sank into the seat at her desk. *It seems like I'm always in trouble. Why do I make so many mistakes?*

As Rachel headed home from school that afternoon, she fretted and fumed. She'd not only had to stay in from recess today, but Elizabeth had made her stay after school to clean the blackboards and sweep the floor.

Jacob hadn't waited for her, either. He'd said he had better things to do.

"That's fine with me," Rachel muttered. "At least I don't have to listen to him scolding me for being late to school and calling me a little bensel."

When Rachel entered her yard, she saw clothes on the line, flapping in the breeze. Mom stood on the back porch, tapping her foot and staring at the porch floor.

"What's wrong, Mom?" Rachel asked as she climbed the porch steps. "You look umgerrent."

"I am upset." *Tap! Tap! Tap!* Mom tapped her foot some more and pointed to the floor. "See this mess the *hinkel* [chickens] made with their droppings?"

Rachel nodded.

"Well, they made that mess because someone left the door to the chicken coop open this morning." Mom peered at Rachel over the top of her glasses. "What do you have to say for yourself, Rachel?"

Rachel gulped. "Well, I—uh—was in a hurry when I left the coop, so I—uh—guess I must have forgotten to shut the door."

"How many times have I told you to close the door to the coop?" Mom asked.

"Lots of times."

Tap! Tap! Tap! "I shouldn't have to keep reminding you, Rachel." *Tap! Tap! Tap!* "You want to be grown up, yet you act like a bensel."

Tears stung Rachel's eyes. It was bad enough that Jacob called her a little bensel. Did Mom have to call her that, too?

"And another thing happened because you left the door open," Mom said. "Some of the chickens ate the cat's food." She pointed to the porch. "I want you to clean up the mess and then get busy on your homework."

Rachel shuffled into the house to get the mop and a bucket of water. This really had not been a good day!

When Rachel climbed into bed that night, she expected to find clean, sweet-smelling sheets since Mom had done laundry. But she discovered her sheets were the same ones as the night before—they looked dirty and wrinkled. They didn't smell fresh and clean, either.

That's strange, she thought. *I saw clothes on the line, so I know Mom did the laundry today. Why didn't she wash my sheets?*

Rachel hurried across the room and opened her closet door. She reached for a clean dress to have all ready for school the next day. But all her dresses were on the floor in a heap.

"Ach, now I remember! This morning Mom asked me to put my dirty clothes in the laundry basket." Rachel frowned. She knew that part of her problem was not listening carefully to Mom. The other part of the problem was that she got sidetracked easily and forgot important things.

"Now I'll have to sleep in dirty, smelly sheets," she grumbled. "Worse yet, tomorrow I'll have to wear a dirty, wrinkled dress to school."

After school the next day, Rachel headed to the greenhouse to see if Grandpa needed any help.

"Have you done your homework yet?" Grandpa asked, his bushy eyebrows pulling together.

Rachel nodded. "I only had a little bit, and I did it right after I ate a snack."

"All right. I'd be happy to have your help."

"What would you like me to do?" Rachel asked.

Grandpa motioned to the broom leaning against the wall. "I spilled some potting soil a few minutes ago. Would you please sweep that up for me?"

"Jah, sure." Rachel grabbed the broom. *Swish! Swish! Swish!* She swept up the dirt in no time at all.

When she put the broom away, she noticed the book about wildflowers lying on a shelf, so she asked Grandpa if she could look at it.

Grandpa nodded. "But only while you're here in the greenhouse. I don't want you to take it outside or even up to the house."

"Okay."

Ding! Ding! The bell above the greenhouse door jingled, and an elderly English couple stepped in. While Grandpa waited on them, Rachel decided to try making a bookmark, following the directions in the wildflower book.

She opened it and frowned as she stared at the page. *I'll need some flowers in order to make this bookmark, and the ones I'm pressing in my room aren't ready yet. I wonder. . .*

Rachel glanced at Grandpa, but he was still busy with his customers. She moved to the shelf where some African violets were and plucked off a few purple blossoms. *I'm sure Grandpa won't mind if I thin a couple of these plants,* she decided as she picked a few more blossoms.

Rachel set to work making her bookmark, gluing each flower petal on an index card she'd cut in half. Then she covered it with clear contact paper, only it didn't look right. It looked kind of lumpy. "Hmm. . . . I wonder if I made a mistake."

She read the directions again. "Cut the index card

in half lengthwise. Arrange the pressed flowers in whatever design you like." Rachel slapped the side of her head. "I needed pressed flowers, not fresh ones. I made a big mistake!"

"What mistake is that?" Grandpa asked, stepping up to Rachel.

She pointed to the bulky bookmark. "I tried making this with fresh flower petals instead of dried ones, and it turned out wrong."

Grandpa tugged his beard. "And just where did you get these fresh flowers?"

"I took them from a couple of African violet plants over there." Rachel pointed to the other side of the room.

Grandpa frowned. "You should have asked first, Rachel. If you'd asked, I would have told you which plants you could pick flowers from."

He glanced at the bookmark. "This would have looked better if you'd used pressed flowers, because the moisture needs to be taken out of a flower blossom for it to lie flat."

"I figured that out after it was too late," Rachel said.

"This is what happens when you do things without asking."

Rachel sniffed. "I'm sorry, Grandpa."

Grandpa gave Rachel a hug. "Just try to do the right thing, okay?"

Rachel nodded. "I don't like making mistakes, and I promise I'll try to do better."

Chapter 7

Aunt Rachel

On the first Saturday morning in October, Pap came into the house with a huge smile on his face.

"I checked our answering machine in the phone shed. There was a message from Rudy," Pap said. He hung his straw hat on a wall peg near the door and sat at the kitchen table.

Mom sipped her cup of tea. "What'd the message say?"

Pap's smile stretched even wider. "Esther had her boppli last night, and it's a buwe! Rudy said Esther and the boppli will come home from the hospital this morning."

Mom set her cup down and jumped up from the table. "*Alli mudder muss sariye fer ihre famiyle* [Every mother has to take care of her family]! I need to get over there right away, because I'm sure she'll need my help."

Mom looked at Rachel, who was sitting at the table writing a letter to Mary. "Do you know what this means?" Mom asked.

Rachel smiled and nodded. "It means I'm an aunt."

Rachel figured being an aunt would make her seem grown up in her family's eyes. Jacob might even stop calling her a little bensel.

Mom patted the top of Rachel's head. "Jah, that, too, but it also means if I go to help Esther today, I'll need your help here."

Rachel's smile turned upside down. "Can't I go over to Esther's with you?"

Mom shook her head. "You need to stay here and take care of Hannah."

"Can't she go with us to Esther's?"

"It'll be easier for me to help Esther if I don't have Hannah to care for, too," Mom said.

Rachel frowned. "Do you expect me to take care of Hannah all by myself?"

Mom nodded. "There are several bottles of milk in the refrigerator and a fresh supply of clean diapers on the dresser in my room. I'm sure you'll do just fine." She patted Rachel's head again. "If you want to be grown up, this will give you a chance to prove it."

Rachel's heart sank all the way to her toes. She did want her family to think she was growing up, but she'd planned to do other things today. Watching Hannah wasn't one of them!

"I shouldn't be gone more than a few hours," Mom said. "But if you need anything, just ask one of the menfolk, because I think they'll be around most of the day." Mom grabbed her jacket and black outer bonnet and started for the door. Then she halted. "I'd better check on Hannah before I go."

Rachel let her head fall forward onto the table and groaned. She wondered if she'd ever get to go over to Esther's to see her new nephew.

I may as well finish this letter to Mary, Rachel decided. *If I don't do it now, I'll probably be so busy watching Hannah that I won't get it done at all.*

Pap pushed his chair away from the table and stood. "I'm going outside to hitch your mamm's horse to one of our buggies. When I'm done with that, I'll be in the fields working with the boys." He smiled at Rachel. "Ring the dinner bell when it's time for lunch, and if you should need anything, you can ring the bell for that, too. Oh, and if Esther feels up to company, we'll all go over there tomorrow after church to see the new boppli."

"Okay," Rachel said as Pap stepped out the door.

A few minutes later, Mom rushed back into the room. "The baby carriage is in the yard," she told Rachel. "The sun's shining, so I'd like you to take Hannah for a ride around the yard so she can get some fresh air."

"I'll do it as soon as I finish this letter," Rachel said as she concentrated on what she wanted to say to Mary. Now she really had some good news to share— she'd become an aunt!

"Okay, and do the best that you can today," Mom said as the door clicked shut behind her.

Rachel hurried to finish Mary's letter; then she left the kitchen and went into Mom and Pap's room to get Hannah.

"Okay, little sister; we're going outside for some fresh air," she said as she walked to the crib.

She halted, and her heart pounded. Hannah wasn't there!

Think, Rachel, think, Rachel told herself. *Let's see now. . . . Mom said I should take Hannah for a ride in her carriage, so maybe Mom put Hannah in the carriage before she left.*

Rachel raced out of the room, grabbed a jacket, and ran out the back door. Sure enough, Hannah's baby carriage sat in the yard. What a relief!

Rachel grabbed the handle and started pushing the carriage around the yard. She pushed and pushed and pushed some more, until she got tired and was completely bored.

"It's time to go back in the house now, Hannah." Rachel bent over the carriage, pulled the blanket aside, and gasped. Hannah wasn't there! Rachel felt so foolish when she realized that she'd been pushing around an empty carriage! *Could someone have come into the yard while I was still in the house and taken Hannah?* she wondered.

Rachel's heart pounded so hard she could hear it

echo in her head. She was getting ready to head to the greenhouse to tell Grandpa what had happened when she heard a faint cry. She tilted her head and listened. The cry sounded like it was coming from inside the house.

Rachel ran up the porch steps two at a time, jerked the door open, and rushed into the house.

Waaa! Waaa! The closer Rachel got to the living room, the louder the crying became. She spotted Hannah's cradle across the room and raced to it. There lay Hannah, with a red face from kicking and screaming.

"It's okay, Hannah," Rachel said as she sat in the chair next to the cradle. She rocked the cradle with her foot, hoping to keep the baby from fussing. She was glad none of her family had been there to see the foolish mistake she'd made. *I should have listened better to Mom*, Rachel thought. *She must have told me that Hannah was in her cradle and that the baby carriage was outside.*

Waaa! Waaa!

Rachel picked up the baby, sat in the rocking chair, and put Hannah in her lap. Rachel patted Hannah's back until she stopped crying. Rachel smiled as she began to rock and hum.

Hannah's eyelids fluttered, and soon she was fast asleep.

Rachel carried Hannah to Mom and Pap's room,

where she put her to bed in her crib.

Now maybe I can do something fun. I think I'll paint a few animals on some of my rocks, Rachel thought as she tiptoed out of the room. *When I'm done with those, I might make some bookmarks with the flowers I've pressed.*

Rachel went to the kitchen and had just placed her paints and some newspaper on the table when Hannah started to howl.

Waaa! Waaa! Waaa!

Rachel looked at the clock. Only five minutes had passed since she'd put Hannah in her crib, and already she was crying. *Maybe if I ignore her, she'll go back to sleep,* Rachel thought as she picked up her paintbrush.

Waaa! Waaa! Hannah's crying got louder.

Rachel's chair scraped against the floor as she pushed away from the table with a groan. "Always trouble somewhere!"

When Rachel entered Mom and Pap's room, she first checked Hannah's diaper. Sure enough, it was sopping wet. She looked for the diaper pail but didn't see it. Then she remembered that Mom sometimes rinsed the baby's diapers in the toilet, so she carried the diaper into the bathroom and dropped it into the toilet bowl.

"*Windle wesche gleich ich net* [I don't like to wash out diapers]," Rachel said as she bounced the diaper up and down.

Waaa! Waaa! Hannah screamed even louder. Her

cries seemed to bounce off the walls. Rachel dropped the diaper into the toilet and gritted her teeth, trying not to cry herself. She hoped she could get Hannah settled down soon so she could paint those rocks.

She hurried back to the bedroom and quickly put a clean diaper on the baby. "There, that's better isn't it, Hannah?"

Waaa! Waaa!

Maybe she's hungry, Rachel thought. She stroked the baby's flushed cheeks. "I'll go to the kitchen and get you a bottle of milk. I'll be right back."

Rachel raced into the kitchen. Then she opened the refrigerator and took out one of the baby bottles Mom had filled with milk. She placed the bottle into a kettle of water and turned on the stove. Every few seconds she tipped the bottle upside down and let some milk drip onto her wrist to test it. When it felt lukewarm, she knew it was ready for Hannah.

When Rachel returned to the bedroom, Hannah was still crying and kicking her feet. Rachel set the bottle on the nightstand by Mom's side of the bed. Then she picked Hannah up, sat in the rocking chair, and put the bottle in Hannah's mouth.

Hannah quit crying, and her little lips went in and out as she sucked on the milk.

When the bottle was empty, Rachel lifted Hannah to her shoulder and patted her back. After several pats, Hannah let out a loud burp!

Rachel was relieved that Hannah had burped so quickly. Usually it didn't happen so fast.

Rachel rose from her chair and was heading down the hall with Hannah when Henry came into the house.

"Did you need something?" Rachel asked her brother.

"Just using the bathroom." Henry smiled at Rachel. "Then I'll refill my thermos with coffee and take it out to the fields. Everything going okay?"

"Jah. I'm going to put Hannah in her cradle, and then I'll be in the kitchen painting rocks," Rachel said as she started for the living room.

Rachel had just gotten Hannah settled in her cradle when Henry hollered, "Who left a windel in the toilet?"

"Oh no." Rachel's palms grew sweaty as she raced from the room. "I hope you didn't flush that diaper down the toilet!"

When Henry stepped out of the bathroom, his face was bright red. "Did you put that windel in the toilet?" he asked Rachel.

She nodded. "I put it there so I could rinse it out. I've seen Mom do it."

"Well, she doesn't walk away and leave it there." A little vein on the side of Henry's head stuck out. "If I'd have flushed the toilet, that windel could've gotten stuck and clogged the drain. You really ought to grow up and learn to be more responsible!" He frowned at Rachel and slowly shook his head.

"I was going to get the diaper, but Hannah started fussing, and I sort of forgot it was there." Rachel swallowed a couple of times. She felt like she'd swallowed a glob of sticky peanut butter that wouldn't go down.

"You seem to have a short attention span lately," Henry said.

Rachel stared at the floor as she struggled not to cry. "I do not; I just have a lot on my mind. Besides, it's perfectly normal for people to forget sometimes."

"Well, get your head out of the clouds and start paying better attention!"

Rachel's shoulders started to shake. She dropped her head into her hands as she gave in to her tears.

"Oh, now, don't start crying on me." Henry patted Rachel's trembling shoulder. "I'm sorry for yelling, but if you're going to take care of the boppli, you need to pay close attention to what you're doing."

Sniff! Sniff! Rachel swiped at the tears rolling down her cheeks. "I'm trying to be grown up, but it seems like no matter how hard I try, I always mess up."

Henry gave Rachel's shoulder another pat. "I'm sure you'll grow up someday. But in the meantime, go get that windel out of the toilet."

Chapter 8

Gone Fishing

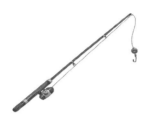

"It's cold out there this morning. I think it might snow," Rachel said as she dashed into the kitchen the next morning. She'd just finished feeding the chickens.

Jacob, who'd followed Rachel into the house, grunted and rolled his eyes. "It's not going to snow, little bensel. It's too early for that."

Mom turned from the stove and frowned. "Stop calling your sister a silly child, Jacob."

Meow! Hiss! Hiss! Meow!

Rachel jumped when her cats raced into the house, bumped into her leg, and slid across the kitchen floor.

"Ach! Who let those cats in?" Mom asked with a frown.

"Jacob did!"

"Rachel did!"

Rachel and Jacob had spoken at the same time.

"Look, the door's open!" Rachel pointed to the back door; then she pointed to Jacob. "You were the last one in, so you must not have shut it."

Jacob glared at Rachel. "It's your fault because you started talking about the cold weather and said it might snow."

Rachel frowned as she shook her head. "What's that have to do with anything? You left the door open; that's all there is to it!"

"Oh, grow up, Rachel, and quit trying to put the blame on me."

"I'll grow up when I'm good and ready!"

Mom stepped between them. "It doesn't matter who left the door open. You need to capture those two crazy critters running around my kitchen!"

"I'll get Cuddles!" Jacob shouted as he dashed across the room after the cat.

"I'll get Snowball!" Rachel hollered.

Hiss! Hiss! Yeow! Cuddles darted across the floor and swooped under Grandpa's legs when he entered the kitchen.

Grandpa teetered unsteadily and grabbed the back of a chair. "Wh–what's going on in here?"

"Rachel's cats are loose and we're trying to catch 'em," Jacob yelled as he ran down the hall after Cuddles.

Snowball raced into the living room, and Rachel followed.

Meow! The kitten leaped into Hannah's cradle.

Waaa! Waaa! Hannah wailed.

"Snowball, no!" Rachel grabbed the kitten by the scruff of its neck and raced out of the room. She was almost to the back door when Jacob came running down the hall holding Cuddles in his arms.

"We'd better get them outside before there's any more trouble," Rachel panted.

Jacob nodded, and they both hurried out the door.

When they returned to the kitchen, Mom was back at the stove, and Grandpa was sitting at the table holding Hannah.

"That bussli of yours scared our Hannah," Grandpa said to Rachel.

She nodded. "She's okay, isn't she? I don't think Snowball scratched her or anything."

Grandpa kissed the top of Hannah's head. "She seems fine to me."

Just then, Pap and Henry came in from doing their chores.

Whoosh! Cuddles streaked into the room, with Snowball right behind her.

"Levi, you forgot to shut the door!" Mom shook her finger at Pap like he was a little boy. "We've already dealt with those crazy cats once this morning. Must we do it again?"

Pap's face turned red. "Sorry, Miriam. I didn't realize I'd left the door open."

Meow! Hiss! Meow! The cats raced around the room as if their tails were on fire.

"I'll get Cuddles!" Jacob shouted.

"I'll get Snowball," Rachel said.

They both took off after the cats, hollering and waving their arms.

By the time they got the cats outside again, Rachel was exhausted. She was glad it wasn't her fault that they'd gotten in the house this time. It was nice to know she wasn't the only one who got in trouble with Mom.

Rachel chuckled. She could hardly believe it, but even Pap had been scolded by Mom this morning.

"Could you get me a carton of eggs?" Mom asked Rachel. "I need a few more, because your daed likes to have three."

"Okay, Mom." Rachel scooted to the refrigerator, removed the carton of eggs, and handed it to Mom.

"Just set it on the counter." Mom took out the eggs she'd been frying and placed them on a plate. Then she reached for an egg from the carton. The oil in the pan sizzled, and Mom wasn't watching what she was doing as she cracked the egg and dropped it in the pan. A horrible smell rose from the pan and made the whole room stink.

"Eww. . .that was a rotten egg!" Mom turned to Rachel and frowned. "Apparently you haven't been checking for eggs very well."

Rachel frowned. She knew she was supposed to check the chicken coop carefully. Sometimes if an egg was hidden for days, it would be rotten when it was found.

Mom grabbed the frying pan with a pot holder and hauled it to the garbage can. Then she dumped the egg in the can and handed it to Rachel. "Please take this outside and dump it in the trash can. And from now on, when you're asked to check for eggs, be sure you look in every nesting box and anywhere else in the coop that the chickens might lay their eggs."

Rachel held her breath as she lugged the garbage outside. From now on she'd try to do better about checking for eggs.

After church that afternoon, Rachel's family headed down the road in their buggy. They were on their way to Esther and Rudy's to see the new baby. Even Grandpa and Grandma Yoder went along, only they rode with Uncle Amos, Aunt Karen, and their little boy, Gerald.

When the Yoders arrived, Rachel was the first one to jump out of the buggy. "I'll meet you at the house," she called to Mom as she raced across the lawn.

When she entered Esther's house, she found Esther and Rudy sitting on the sofa in the living room. Esther held a baby in her arms.

"Well, Aunt Rachel," Esther said with a wide smile, "what do you think of your new nephew, Ben?"

Rachel looked at the baby. His face was bright pink

and kind of wrinkly. Unlike Hannah, who was born with pretty blond hair, little Ben had no hair at all!

Rachel wasn't sure what to say. She didn't think "cute" quite fit this baby, but she wanted to say something nice. "He—uh—is sure little."

"Jah, he's that all right," Rudy said with a nod. "But I'm sure he'll grow up fast."

Ben opened his blue-gray eyes and worked his tiny mouth, making a strange snuffling noise.

Soon the rest of Rachel's family entered the room. Everyone started talking at once, making silly sounds and wanting to hold the new baby.

Rachel moved over to stand near the fireplace. She'd finally realized that all babies got a lot of attention when they were young. But when they got older, folks didn't fuss over them so much. Rachel figured in a few years, neither Hannah nor little Ben would be the center of attention. They'd both have a bunch of chores to do and be told to keep quiet if they made too much noise.

"Kumme! Kumme!" Gerald said, tugging on Rachel's hand. "Horsey ride!"

"No." Rachel shook her head so hard the ties on her kapp flipped in her face. "The last time I gave you a horsey ride, you poked me in the eye."

Gerald's lower lip jutted out, and his eyes filled with tears. "Horsey ride!"

"Why don't you and Gerald work on a puzzle

together?" Esther suggested. "There's one in the bottom drawer of Rudy's desk, and it's fairly easy."

Rachel wasn't in the mood to put a puzzle together, but she figured it would be better than turning herself into a horse so Gerald could kick her in the side. "Jah, okay," she said, taking Gerald's hand and leading him to Rudy's desk.

When she found the puzzle, she dumped the pieces on the floor and told Gerald to sit down.

While they worked on the puzzle, Rachel listened to the grown-ups talk.

"Now, Esther," Mom said, "don't try to do too much too soon. The boppli will keep you up at night for several weeks, so rest as much as you can, whenever you have the chance. I'll come over tomorrow afternoon to fix supper for you and Rudy."

Mom turned to Rachel and said, "Be sure you come straight home from school tomorrow, because I'll need you to watch Hannah while I come over here."

Rachel nodded and reached for a puzzle piece.

The next morning, Rachel headed to the coop to gather eggs before breakfast. She was in a hurry and didn't want to be late for school, so she hurried to feed and water the chickens and decided not to check all the nesting the boxes.

I can check them after school, she decided. *Mom said we're just having cold cereal this morning, and she doesn't need any eggs for that.*

Then she remembered the horrible smell the rotten egg had made in the kitchen, so she turned around and thoroughly checked each nesting box.

Carrying a basket full of eggs, Rachel hurried back to the house, anxious to eat breakfast and head for school.

As Rachel and her family sat around the table, Mom turned to Rachel and said, "Now don't forget, Rachel, I need you to come straight home from school this afternoon."

"Why?" Rachel asked.

"Because I want you to watch Hannah while I go over to help at Esther and Rudy's. I mentioned this to you yesterday, remember?"

"Oh yeah; I guess so," Rachel mumbled around a spoonful of cereal.

After school, Jacob went to see Orlie, and Rachel, excited to see if Grandpa needed any help today, headed straight for the greenhouse. She was surprised to find the door locked, and even more surprised when she discovered a note tacked on the door that read "Gone fishing."

Rachel frowned. She'd been looking forward to smelling the greenhouse scents, watering some plants, and helping Grandpa with whatever he needed.

Maybe I should go fishing, too, she decided. *Mom said*

something about her taking Hannah and going over to Esther's place, so she shouldn't need me for anything. Even so, I guess I should leave a note.

Rachel set her backpack on the ground, took out a pencil, and wrote on Grandpa's note: "Rachel went fishing, too." Then she ran to the shed where everyone's fishing gear was kept and took out her pole. After that, she dug several worms, put them in a can, and headed across the field toward their neighbor's pond.

When Rachel arrived at the pond, she expected to see Grandpa, but there was no sign of him. *Maybe he went fishing somewhere else,* she thought as she sat on a fallen log.

Rachel baited her hook, threw her line into the water, leaned her head back, and stared at the puffy clouds overhead. Today was a warm fall day—nothing like the cold weather they'd had lately.

She closed her eyes and let the sun warm her face as she imagined a nice big fish tugging on the end of her line.

Woof! Woof!

Rachel's eyes snapped open. She turned just in time to see Buddy running across the field toward her.

"Oh no," she moaned. "That overgrown mutt's gonna scare away all the fish!"

Woof! Woof! Whomp! Buddy bounded up to Rachel so hard that he knocked her off the log, and—

splash!—she landed right in the water!

She came up sputtering and hollering, "You stupid mutt! I'll get you for this!"

Buddy took off like a flash, heading in the direction of home.

Rachel's teeth chattered as she clambered out of the chilly water. So much for an afternoon of fishing!

She gathered her things and started for the house. She'd only made it halfway there when she met Grandpa. "Where have you been, Rachel, and why are your clothes sopping wet?"

"I—I saw the n–note you left on the greenhouse d–door and decided to j–join you for some f–fishing." By now Rachel was shivering so badly that she could hardly talk.

"We need to get you back home and into some dry clothes," Grandpa said.

"O–okay." Rachel hurried along. "Where were you, Grandpa? I th–thought you were going f–fishing."

"I was. I went over to the Burkholders' place and fished in that big pond behind their pasture." Grandpa lifted a bucket full of fish. "I've got plenty of fish for us to have for supper tonight."

He stopped walking and looked at Rachel with a strange expression. "Say, if you're here with me, then who's up at the house watching Hannah?"

"W–what?" Rachel's lips were so cold she could barely move them.

"Your mamm was going over to Esther and Rudy's

to help them and fix their supper. She wanted you to babysit Hannah, remember?"

"Oh no," Rachel groaned. "I th–thought that—" She clamped her mouth shut and started to run. "I'm gonna be in b–big trouble for this!"

When Rachel entered the house, she was greeted by Mom, who didn't look happy. "Where have you been, Rachel, and why—" She stopped talking in midsentence and stared at Rachel's dress. "Is it raining outside?"

Rachel shook her head. "I—uh—fell in the p–pond when Buddy knocked me into the w–water."

Mom's mouth formed an O. "What were you doing at the pond when you were supposed to be here watching Hannah?"

"I forgot about w–watching Hannah, and I w–went fishing instead." Rachel hung her head, unable to look Mom in the eye. She'd messed up again, big time!

"When are you going to grow up and stop being so forgetful?" Mom asked as she led Rachel into the kitchen.

"I—I don't know. I want to be g–grown up, but—" *Ah-choo! Ah-choo!* Rachel grabbed a napkin from the basket on the kitchen table and blew her nose. "I th–think I might be getting a cold."

"Let's get you out of those wet clothes and into a warm bath," Mom said, guiding Rachel down the hall toward the bathroom. "I need to get to Esther's right now, but I'll get some hot water going on the stove before I go. You can make yourself a cup of tea after your bath."

"Wh—what about Hannah? Who's g–going to watch her?" Rachel wanted to know.

"I'll watch Hannah," Grandpa said as he joined them in the hall. "I can keep an eye on her while I clean my fish."

"Danki, Dad," Mom said, giving Grandpa a quick hug. Then she turned to Rachel and said, "Into the bathroom with you now. We can talk about your poor memory after I get home."

When Rachel headed down the hall, she thought to herself, *I wish I'd never gone fishing!*

Chapter 9
Total Chaos

Rachel pressed her nose to the window and watched as Mom got into the buggy. Dad handed Hannah to her. Then he went around to the driver's side and got in, too.

It's not fair, Rachel thought as she watched the horse and buggy move down the driveway toward the road. *They should have let me go to town with them.*

She sniffed a couple of times. *They shouldn't make me stay home and clean house all day just because I forgot about watching Hannah the other day.*

"*Es fenschder muss mer nass mache fer es sauwer mache* [One has to wet the window in order to clean it]," Grandpa said when he entered the living room. "Looks to me like you're putting more smudges on the window with the end of your *naas* [nose]."

Rachel pulled back and stared at the window. Sure enough, there was a smudge where her nose had been. "I was just watching Pap's buggy head down the road and wishing I could have gone with them," she said with a sigh.

"You know why you can't go," Grandpa said.

She nodded and swallowed.

Grandpa put his hand on Rachel's shoulder. "It's never fun to be punished, but that's how we learn from our mistakes." He gave her shoulder a gentle squeeze. "Besides, a little hard work never hurt anyone."

"That's right," Henry said as he entered the room. "Those who work hard eat hearty!"

Rachel frowned. "I never said anything about eating."

Henry shrugged and headed for the door. "I'm going over to see my *aldi* [girlfriend], Nancy," he said, turning to look at Grandpa. "If Mom and Pap get back before I do, tell Mom I won't be home for supper."

"I'll be sure to tell her," Grandpa said with a nod.

Just then, Jacob entered the room with a wide smile.

"Why are you so happy?" Rachel asked as she squirted some liquid cleaner on the window.

"Orlie got a new scooter the other day, and I'm going over to ride on it."

"Well, have fun," Rachel mumbled under her breath. "I sure won't have any fun here."

"What was that?" Jacob asked as he moved toward the door.

"Oh, nothing." Rachel wiped the window with the

clean cloth and stood back to take a look. She was glad when Jacob went out the door without saying anything else to her.

"You missed a spot," Grandpa said, pointing to the left side of the window.

Psshheew! Psshheew! Rachel shot some more cleaner on the window and wiped the cloth over it again. Cleaning the house was boring. No fun at all on a Saturday morning!

Rachel moved away from the window and picked up the dust cloth she'd laid on the coffee table. "Work, work, work!" she grumbled as she wiped the cloth carelessly over the table. "That's all I'm good for anymore. I never get to do anything fun at all!"

"You're never too young or too old to be God's helper," Grandpa said as he lowered himself into his rocking chair.

"I'm not helping God, Grandpa," Rachel said. "I'm helping Mom."

Grandpa reached for his Bible on the small table by his chair. He opened it to a place that had been marked with a long white ribbon. "I mentioned this verse from the *Biewel* [Bible] to you several weeks ago, but I want to read it to you now, so please have a seat," he said, motioning to the sofa.

Rachel sat down with a weary sigh.

Grandpa picked up his reading glasses from the table and slipped them on. Then he began to read:

" 'Whatever you do, work at it with all your heart, as working for the Lord, not for men.' " He smiled. "That's in Colossians 3:23."

Rachel sat still for several seconds, staring at the floor and letting the words Grandpa had read sink into her brain. Finally, she looked up at Grandpa and said, "I guess if the work I'm doing is for the Lord, then I'd better get busy."

Deciding this was a good chance to show that she was grown up, Rachel rose to her feet. Then she bent down and picked up the braided throw rug in front of Pap's favorite chair and hauled it outside to the porch.

Honk! Honk! Honk!

Rachel dropped the rug onto the porch and stepped into the yard to watch a flock of geese fly over the house in a perfect V formation. She wished she could fly away, too—at least for today.

When the geese disappeared, Rachel stepped back onto the porch, picked up the rug, and shook it well. She would do the best that she could so she would please the Lord.

When the rug was as clean as she could get it, Rachel went back in the house. She left the rug in the hallway then went to the utility room to get a broom.

When Rachel returned to the living room, she started sweeping hard. *Swish! Swish! Swish!* Bits of dust flew up and tickled her nose.

They must have tickled Grandpa's nose, too, for he

soon began to sneeze. *Ah-choo! Ah-choo! Ah-choo!* Rachel kept count. Grandpa sneezed eight times in all.

She giggled and giggled and giggled some more. Grandpa's sneezes sounded so funny, she couldn't help but giggle.

When Grandpa finally quit sneezing, he started laughing, too. "All that dust you were sweeping must have gotten to me, Rachel."

Rachel's smile faded. "I'm sorry about that, Grandpa. I didn't mean to make you sneeze."

"It's okay. The floor needed to be cleaned." Grandpa smiled. "Now I'm going to give you an object lesson."

"What's that?" Rachel asked.

He motioned to one corner of the room. "Look over there. Do you see any dust in the air?"

"No," Rachel said with a shake of her head.

Grandpa pointed toward the window. "Now look at the sunlight coming through the window glass. What do you see there?"

"I see a lot of dust particles where the sun's shining through."

Grandpa nodded. "It's just like God's Word."

Rachel tipped her head. "What do you mean?"

"When the light of His Word shines on us, it reveals the sin in our lives."

"Hmm. . ." Rachel stared at the dust particles as she thought about this.

"When we have sin in our lives, we have to sweep it away by asking God to forgive us."

Rachel nodded and a lump formed in her throat. She knew it was a sin whenever she disobeyed her parents or teacher. She bowed her head and closed her eyes. *Dear God, forgive my sins and help me to do better from now on.*

When she opened her eyes, she smiled at Grandpa and said, "I think I'll clean the kitchen and bathroom next. Then I'll head upstairs and clean my bedroom."

Grandpa smiled. "That's a good idea, Rachel. I'm pleased to see you working so hard today, and I'm sure that God is, too."

Rachel grabbed the broom and skipped out of the room.

By noon, Rachel was hot, tired, and hungry. She'd just finished scrubbing the bathroom floor and her back had begun to ache. She straightened up and rubbed at the kinks in her back. She was so tired of cleaning. She just wanted to go upstairs, lie down on her bed, and read a good book.

Her stomach rumbled noisily, reminding her that she needed to prepare lunch for Grandpa and herself. Grandpa was probably feeling hungry, too.

"I'm going into the kitchen to fix us something to eat," she called as she passed the living room on her way to the kitchen.

No response.

Rachel poked her head into the living room. Grandpa's head leaned against the back of the rocking chair. His eyes were closed, and his mouth hung slightly open. Several loud snores escaped his lips.

Rachel figured he would probably sleep for a while, so she headed upstairs to rest a few minutes before starting lunch. After she ate, she would clean her room.

When she entered her bedroom, she froze. Jacob's big shaggy mutt was on her bed, sitting in the middle of her rumpled sheets. She'd forgotten to make her bed this morning.

"I have no idea how you got in here," she said, shaking her finger at Buddy, "but you're not taking a nap on my *bett* [bed]!"

She waved her hands, but Buddy didn't budge. He just sat staring at Rachel as if to say, "I'm staying here, and you can't make me move."

Rachel gritted her teeth. "Get off my bett, you hairy beast!" She hoped if she let him know she meant business, he might obey her for a change.

Woof! Woof! Buddy lunged for Rachel and licked her arm with his big wet tongue. Then he slid off the bed, knocking the quilt on the floor and pulling the sheets, which had somehow gotten wrapped around his body.

Rachel screamed and grabbed one end of the

sheet as Buddy tore out of the room. She hung on for dear life as the troublesome mutt ran down the stairs, dragging her and the sheet behind him.

"Absatz! Stop, right now!" Rachel hollered. "You're making it hard for me to act grown up!"

Thump! Thump! Thump! Rachel thumped and bumped her way down the stairs, still clinging to the sheet.

When Buddy reached the bottom of the stairs, he plodded into the living room, thumping and bumping everything in sight. Then he raced into the kitchen, barking and growling all the way!

Thud! One of the chairs at the table fell over. *Thunk! Thunk!* Buddy slammed into the table, knocking the bowl of sugar over and sending the napkins sailing through the air.

"Bad dog!" Rachel hollered. "Stop where you are, right now!"

Woof! Woof! Buddy tore out of the kitchen and down the hall, pulling Rachel along on her backside.

When they got to the end of the hall, he turned and raced back again.

"Let go of my sheet, you crazy critter!" Rachel hollered.

"What's all this ruckus about?" Grandpa asked, stepping out of the living room.

Woof! Woof! Buddy whipped past Grandpa at lightning speed. Rachel hung on for all she was worth.

No flea-bitten mutt was going to get the best of her! She would get that sheet back no matter what!

"*Was in der welt* [What in all the world]?" Mom asked as she entered the house. Pap was right behind her, holding Hannah.

Woof! Woof! Buddy raced out the open door, dragging Rachel behind him. *Rip!*—the sheet came loose from Buddy's body, leaving a big tear in one end.

Rachel gasped as she fell on the ground. "No! No! No! You are nothing but a big bag of trouble, Buddy!"

Buddy slunk off toward his doghouse with his tail between his legs.

"Out of sight, out of mind," Rachel mumbled as she picked herself up and brushed off her dress.

Mom rushed out of the house, stepped up to Rachel, and frowned. "Rachel Yoder, I left you home to clean the house. I sure didn't expect to come home and find you playing with Jacob's dog!"

Rachel shook her head. "I wasn't playing with Buddy. That big hairy beast got up on my bed, and then—"

"You know you're not allowed to have any pets on your bed," Mom said. "How many times have I told you that?"

Rachel's chin trembled as she struggled not to cry. "Many times, but—"

"You're never going to grow up if you don't learn to be more responsible," Pap said when he joined them on the lawn. "You need to pay closer attention to what you're doing."

Determined not to give in to her tears, Rachel quickly explained everything that had happened. "If anything's my fault, it's probably that I left the door open for too long when I was outside shaking the rug."

"She's right, Miriam," Grandpa said, stepping outside. "Rachel worked real hard today. I'm sure she didn't let Jacob's *hund* [dog] in the house on purpose."

Rachel nodded. "No, I sure didn't. I just wanted to do a good job of cleaning the house."

Mom looked like she might say something more on the subject. Instead, she patted Rachel's shoulder and said, "We left town earlier than we'd planned and haven't eaten yet. Why don't the two of us go into the house and see about making some lunch?"

Rachel nodded and followed Mom inside. This had not been a good day. It had been a day of total chaos! She hoped tomorrow would be better.

Chapter 10
Rachel's Pie

Two whole weeks had passed since Rachel had gone fishing when she was supposed to watch Hannah for Mom. She was glad her two weeks of not going anywhere and doing extra chores were finally over. Since today was Saturday and there was no school, Rachel looked forward to doing something fun. She'd wanted to help in the greenhouse this morning, but last night Grandpa had said he didn't have anything for her to do there right now.

Rachel put both elbows on the kitchen counter as she stared out the window.

Maybe I'll go to the barn and see if my cats are there, she thought. *Or I could write Mary a letter on the stationery I made with pressed flowers. Jah, that's what I'll do. She'd probably like to hear about my day of total chaos and how Buddy ruined the sheet on my bed.*

As Rachel continued to gaze out the window, she reached across the cupboard to grab a pen from the basket of writing supplies. *Squish!* She felt something gooey and sticky on her elbow.

"Ach no!" Rachel groaned. "Now look what I've done!" She had put her elbow in the apple pie Mom had made before she'd left for Esther's. At least this time Mom had taken Hannah with her, which meant Rachel had plenty of time to make a new pie before Mom got home.

It can't be that hard to bake another pie, she thought. *I've helped Mom bake some pies before. I'll try to remember what Mom has taught me to do, but if I get stuck, I can always find her recipe book to help me.*

Rachel went to the sink and washed her elbow. Then she scurried to the refrigerator to get more apples but discovered that there were none. *Guess I'll take this ruined pie out to Buddy and pick some more apples from the tree,* Rachel decided. She slipped into her jacket, picked up the pie, and hurried out the door.

Buddy was lying on the roof of his doghouse with his eyes closed and his big old nose stuck between his paws. As soon as Rachel stepped into his dog run, his eyes popped open and he jumped off the roof. *Woof! Woof!* Buddy headed straight for Rachel!

Quickly, she dumped the pie into Buddy's dish and dashed for the gate. Once she was safely outside the door, she stood at the fence and watched Buddy dive into the pie as if it were his last meal.

"Greedy glutton," Rachel said, shaking her head.

"All you do is eat, sleep, and cause a lot of trouble."

Slurp! Slurp! Buddy licked his dog dish clean; then he bounded over to the fence to greet Rachel. *Woof! Woof!*

"Go back to your doghouse and take a nap!" Rachel whirled around and hurried toward the apple tree on the side of the house.

When she got to the tree, she looked up and gasped. It was bare! There wasn't one single apple on any of the branches. Then she remembered that Pap had used the rest of the apples to make a batch of apple cider.

"I need to think," Rachel said out loud. "Do we have any more apple trees in our yard?"

She glanced around. She saw a maple tree, an oak tree, and a walnut tree, but no more apple trees.

Rachel wandered around back and spotted a tree in the pasture. It looked like it had a bunch of red apples growing on it, but they seemed kind of small.

Rachel opened the pasture gate and made sure to shut it. Then she hurried until she came to the tree. Looking up, she could see that it was full of apples! They were a lot smaller than most—in fact, some were barely larger than cherries—but they looked nice and red. She was sure they would work just fine for an apple pie.

Rachel was tempted to climb the tree and pick the apples, but she thought about the broken arm she'd ended up with when she'd climbed a tree to rescue Cuddles.

"I need a ladder and a bucket," she said, racing back across the pasture. She opened the gate and shut it again then headed for the barn. She found a bucket near the door and a small ladder in one corner of the barn. She put the handle of the bucket over her arm and grunted when she tried to pick up the ladder. It was too heavy to carry.

Think, Rachel. Think.

She grabbed the ladder and dragged it out of the barn, across the grass, and into the pasture. She continued to drag it until it was under the apple tree; then she stepped carefully onto the first rung and then another, keeping the bucket over her arm. She reached overhead and picked an apple. *Plunk!* She dropped it into the bucket and reached for a second apple and then a third. *Plunk! Plunk!*

Rachel kept picking until she'd picked sixteen apples. They were sure little, but she figured sixteen small apples would equal eight larger apples.

She climbed down the ladder and started back across the field. She was almost to the gate when old Tom plodded up and nudged her arm with his nose. *Neigh! Neigh!*

Rachel giggled. "I bet I know what you want, boy." She set the bucket on the ground and offered Tom one of the apples.

He took one bite, shook his head a couple of times, and dropped the apple to the ground.

"Well, aren't you the finicky one this morning?" Rachel picked up the apple and held it out to Tom.

Neigh! Neigh! The old horse shook his head and trotted away.

"Guess maybe you've eaten too much hay, and now you're not hungry." Rachel bent down, picked up the bucket, and headed back to the tree. She climbed the ladder again and picked another apple.

When she climbed down, she discovered Snowball sitting in the bucket on top of the apples. She laughed and picked up the kitten.

"You silly bussli," Rachel said, petting Snowball's furry head. "You can't stay in this bucket; I have a pie to bake." She placed Snowball on the ground and hurried out of the pasture. She would put the ladder away after she'd finished baking the pie.

As soon as Rachel entered the kitchen, she turned on the oven to 425 degrees. Then she poured the bucket of apples into the sink and washed them thoroughly. After that, she cut each apple into slices and put all the slices into a bowl with a bit of lemon juice to keep them from turning brown.

Next, she made the piecrust. After that, she took out Mom's recipe book and made the filling according to the directions. Then she mixed it with the apples she'd cut up and poured everything into the crust.

Finally, she placed the pie in the oven, shut the door, and set the timer for fifty minutes.

"Now I think I'll make some bookmarks using the pressed flowers I have in my room," Rachel said. She hurried out of the kitchen and was halfway up the stairs when she remembered that she'd forgotten to take the ladder back to the barn.

"Guess I'd better do it now," she mumbled. "If I don't, I might forget."

Rachel raced out of the house and headed straight for the pasture. The ladder seemed even heavier as she dragged it back to the barn.

By the time Rachel returned to the house, she was tired. *Guess I can make the bookmarks some other time,* she decided.

Rachel flopped into a chair and rested her head on the table. She felt so drowsy.

Ding! Ding! Ding! Rachel's eyes popped open, and she jumped out of her chair. "The pie! I've gotta check on the pie!"

She opened the oven door and stuck a knife into the pie. The apples seemed tender, so she grabbed a pot holder, removed the pie, and placed it on a cooling rack on the counter.

"It looks pretty good," Rachel said, feeling rather pleased with herself. Juice oozed through the piecrust, begging her to taste it, but she summoned her willpower. She needed to wait until it was time to serve the pie for dessert tonight, and she couldn't let on that this wasn't the pie Mom had baked.

Rachel yawned and stretched her arms over her head. Doing grown-up things sure took a lot of work.

"I smell somethin' good," Jacob said as he entered the kitchen through the back door. "What's for lunch?"

"It's an apple pie you smell, and I don't know what's for lunch yet, because I've been busy with other things," Rachel said.

"Are you going to start lunch soon?" he asked.

"I guess so."

"Well, do more than guess so. Grandpa will be in from the greenhouse soon, and he'll be hungry." Jacob marched across the room, took the cookie jar down from the cupboard, and grabbed four peanut butter cookies. Then he turned to Rachel and said, "I'll be outside with Buddy. Call me when lunch is ready."

"You could at least offer to help," Rachel mumbled when the door banged shut behind Jacob. She glanced out the window and saw him heading for Buddy's dog run. When Jacob opened the gate, Buddy ran out, jumped up, and licked Jacob's face. Jacob pushed Buddy down and held out a cookie. Buddy opened his mouth and took a bite; then Jacob popped the rest of the cookie into his own mouth.

Rachel wrinkled her nose. "Yuk! Boys can be so

gross. I'd never let that bad-breathed mutt touch my cookie with his big dirty mouth!"

She turned toward the refrigerator to find something for lunch.

That evening, Esther, Rudy, and their baby came for supper. Little Ben still had no hair, but at least his face wasn't so red and wrinkly anymore. Rachel figured after a few more weeks, he might look almost as cute as Hannah.

"Who's ready for dessert?" Mom asked after the family members had finished their chicken and dumplings.

"I'm pretty full," Rudy said, "but I might have room for a little more. What are we having?"

"I baked an apple pie this morning before I came over to your place," Mom said. She pushed back her chair and started to get up, but Rachel jumped up first.

"I can serve the pie," Rachel said. "Why don't you stay at the table and visit?"

"Are you sure?" Mom peered at Rachel over the top of her glasses. She looked as though she thought Rachel couldn't serve the pie by herself.

"I'm very sure." Rachel hurried across the room and took a knife and pie server from the drawer. Then she pulled back the dish towel covering the pie and cut the pie into eight even pieces. Next, she took eight plates down from the cupboard.

"You're certainly getting tall, Rachel," Esther commented. "You didn't have to reach very far at all to get those plates."

Rachel smiled and stretched herself so she would appear even taller. "I think I've grown almost an inch this week."

"I think you might have at that," Pap said with a chuckle and a twinkle in his eyes. "Jah, Rachel's growing like a weed."

Rachel grinned as she lifted the pieces of pie out of the pan and placed them carefully on the plates. After she'd given everyone some pie, she took a seat at the table.

"Mmm. . .this sure looks good." Rudy took a big bite, and a strange expression came over his face. He grabbed his cup of coffee and quickly swallowed some.

Jacob bit into his piece of pie. "*Agggh*. . . this pie's baremlich!" He jumped out of his chair, rushed over to the garbage, and spit out the pie. Then he grabbed a glass from the cupboard, turned on the water at the sink, and took a big drink.

Mom took a bite of pie and made a horrible face. "This can't be the same pie I made today," she said with a shake of her head. "Something is definitely wrong with this pie."

Rachel slumped in her seat as her face turned warm. She'd blown it again, and she figured she'd better confess right away.

"I baked the pie," she admitted.

Mom's mouth dropped open. "What?"

Rachel quickly explained how she'd put her elbow in Mom's pie and then went out to the pasture and picked some apples so she could make another pie.

"You picked apples from a tree in the pasture?" Pap asked.

Rachel nodded. "They were kind of small, so I had to use sixteen instead of eight."

Pap stared at the piece of pie on his plate; then he looked back at Rachel. "Those apples you picked from the pasture are crabapples, Rachel. They're sour and tart and not meant for baking pies."

"Oh no!" Rachel cried. "How could I have made such a mistake? I'm just a big *dummkopp* [dunce]."

"Now, Rachel, don't be so hard on yourself. Everyone makes mistakes sometimes." Mom patted Rachel's arm. "If you'd told me what happened to my pie as soon as I got home from Esther's, I'd have helped you bake another pie."

"But there were no more apples on the tree in our yard," Rachel said.

"We could have baked some other kind."

"Trouble, trouble, trouble!" Rachel moaned. "My life's always full of trouble!"

"Trouble's like a bubble," Grandpa said. "It soon pops and moves away. Why, I'll bet by tomorrow you'll have forgotten all about the pie you made today."

Rachel sniffed, trying to hold back her tears. "But now we have no dessert."

"I think I can take care of that." Pap rose from his chair. "I'll make a big batch of popcorn, and we'll have some warm apple cider to go with it."

"You didn't make it with crabapples, I hope," said Henry.

Pap shook his head. "Although I've heard that adding a few crabapples to a batch of cider can make the flavor a bit more interesting."

Rachel wrinkled her nose. "I think I'd prefer my cider and pie without any crabapples, thank you very much."

Everyone laughed, even Rachel. She was glad that no one in the family seemed to be mad about the pie she'd ruined.

My day might have started out on a wrong note, she thought, *but it turned out good in the end, and that's all that counts.*

Chapter 11
Bad Advice

Tap! Tap! Tap! "Rachel, are you in there?"

Rachel sighed. She'd just sat on the floor to look at some of the flowers she had pressed, and she didn't want to be disturbed.

"What do you want, Jacob?" she called through her closed door.

"I need to talk to you."

"About what?"

Tap! Tap! Tap! "Can I come in?"

Rachel sighed again. "I suppose."

The door opened, and Jacob stepped into Rachel's room. He raked his fingers through the sides of his hair. "I was wondering if you'd do me a favor."

"What favor?" she asked.

"I need a haircut."

Rachel's eyebrows shot up. "You want me to cut your hair?"

He gave a quick nod.

Rachel shook her head really hard. "I've never cut anyone's hair before. That's Mom's job."

"But Mom's not here. She's been busy helping Esther, and she never has time to cut my hair."

Rachel sat there shaking her head.

Jacob came over and took a seat beside her on the floor. "Come on, Rachel, you can do it. I know you can."

"I—I don't think so. I might mess it up."

"I'm sure you won't. You've seen Mom do it many times. Please, Rachel, it can't be that hard."

"I don't know—"

Jacob touched her arm. "It's just a simple cut. Maybe you could put a bowl on my head and cut around it."

Rachel snickered. "Jah, right, Jacob. Now that would really be *dumm* [dumb]."

He chuckled. "Maybe so, but I'm sure if you just take your time, you can cut my hair with no trouble at all."

"I have trouble with almost everything these days," Rachel said. "I think you should wait until Mom has time to cut your hair."

"She may never have the time," Jacob argued. "Between taking care of Hannah, helping Esther with Ben, and keeping things going around here, she's busier than a bird building a nest."

Rachel couldn't argue with that. Mom was busier

than ever these days, and Rachel had been given a lot more chores to do since Hannah came along.

Jacob shook Rachel's arm. "Will you cut my hair or not?"

"No."

"I'll pay you a quarter."

"That's not enough."

"How about fifty cents?"

"Make it a dollar and I'll do it."

Jacob frowned. "You drive a hard bargain, Rachel. Are you sure you won't do it for less?"

She folded her arms and shook her head.

"Okay, I'll pay you one dollar for cutting my hair." Jacob jumped up. "I'll get the scissors and meet you in the kitchen," he called as he raced out the door.

Rachel groaned and rose to her feet. "I sure hope I don't mess up Jacob's hair."

When Rachel entered the kitchen a few minutes later, she found Jacob sitting in a chair in the middle of the room. A pair of scissors and a comb lay on the counter. He smiled up at her. "Ready?"

"Ready as I'll ever be, I guess." Rachel picked up the comb and ran it through the sides of Jacob's hair.

"What are you doing? You're supposed to be cutting my hair, not combing it," he grumbled.

"I know, but I need to make sure all the ends are straight before I begin." Truthfully, that was only part of the reason Rachel had combed Jacob's hair. She was really stalling for time. "I—uh—need to clean my glasses so I can see clearly what I'm doing."

"Your glasses don't look dirty to me." Jacob grunted. "Just hurry up and get this done. I don't have all day!"

Rachel gritted her teeth and picked up the scissors. It would serve Jacob right if she cut all his hair off and he ended up bald like baby Ben. *Snip! Snip!* She cut one side, and then she moved to the other. *Snip! Snip!*

"Oops!"

"Oops, what?" Jacob's forehead wrinkled. "What'd you do to my hair, Rachel?"

"Uh—the left side looks a little shorter than the right side."

Jacob raced to the mirror hanging on the wall. "It's not so bad," he said, pulling his fingers through the left side of his hair. "All you need to do is cut a little more hair off the right side of my head and everything will be fine."

Rachel wasn't so sure about that, but she nodded and said, "Take a seat."

Jacob plunked down in his chair and turned his head so the right side was facing Rachel.

She picked up the scissors. *Snip! Snip!*

"Oh, oh."

Jacob's eyes widened. "Oh, oh, what, Rachel?"

"Now the right side looks shorter."

"Then take a little more off the left side." Jacob glanced at the clock on the wall. "And hurry up. I don't want to be sitting here all day."

Rachel studied the left side of Jacob's hair; then she studied the right side. She snipped a little here and a little there. Finally, she smiled and said, "I think both sides are even now."

"What about the back? You haven't cut any of that yet," Jacob said.

Rachel moved behind Jacob and lifted the scissors. *Snip! Snip! Snip!*

"Oh no!" she groaned.

"Oh no, what?" Jacob frowned. "What'd you do to my hair, Rachel?"

Rachel shifted from one foot to the other. "Well, I—uh—"

"Just say it, Rachel! Tell me what you did!"

Rachel's chin quivered, and her eyes filled with tears. "Th–there's a chunk of hair missing, and—and it looks real bad."

Jacob touched the back of his head and winced. "Can't you fix it?"

She shook her head. "Not unless you want me to glue it back on."

"Very funny, Rachel." He scowled at her. "Wait until Mom sees what you've done!"

Rachel gulped, wondering what kind of punishment Mom would dish out for this.

"This is what I get for listening to you," she said, pointing at Jacob. "You begged me to cut your hair, and you said it wouldn't be hard." She slowly shook her head. "You gave me some very bad advice!"

Jacob grunted. "You're the one who messed up my hair, so don't blame me. You should have held the scissors steadier and paid closer attention to what you were doing."

Rachel dropped the scissors on the counter and held out her hand. "Where's my money?"

"What money?"

"The money you said you'd pay me for cutting your hair."

Jacob pulled his fingers through the back of his hair and grunted. "You expect me to pay you for messing up my hair?"

Rachel nodded. "You said you would." She figured if she got paid, it might make her feel a little better. After Mom came home and looked at Jacob's hair, Rachel knew she wouldn't feel good about anything.

Jacob marched across the room to the mirror. He turned his head from side to side; then his face got red.

"I can't see what you did to the back of my head," he said, glaring at Rachel, "but I can see what you did to the sides, and they look baremlich!" He grabbed his straw hat from the wall peg and pushed it on his head. "I'll never be able to take my hat off again!"

"Sure you will. . .as soon as your hair grows out."

Rachel held out her hand. "Are you going to pay me or not?"

"No, I'm definitely not!"

"You'd better keep your promise, Jacob Yoder." By now, Rachel's patience had ended. She hadn't wanted to cut Jacob's hair in the first place, but he'd insisted. She wished she hadn't let him talk her into it. What a huge mistake.

"I won't pay you one single cent!" Jacob shouted.

"What's all the yelling about?" Mom asked as she came through the back door with Hannah. "I could hear you two hollering clear out by the buggy shed."

Mom halted, and her mouth dropped open. "Ach, Jacob! What happened to your hair?"

Jacob pointed at Rachel. "She cut it, and now it's ruined!"

Rachel gulped. How could she explain her way out of this? She couldn't fix the mistake she'd made on Jacob's hair, and she sure couldn't hide it, either. "*Er hot mich verschwetzt* [He talked me into it]," she said, pointing at Jacob.

Mom squinted at Jacob as she shifted Hannah to her other arm. "You asked Rachel to cut your hair?"

Jacob's face turned red as he nodded slowly.

"Why'd you do that, Jacob? Why didn't you ask me to cut your hair?" Mom questioned.

"I did ask, but you always said you were too busy." Jacob pointed to his hair. "I didn't think it'd be that hard to cut, so I asked Rachel to do it."

"Actually, he begged me to cut it," Rachel said. "He even promised to give me a dollar if I cut it, but now he won't pay what he owes."

Mom's eyebrows furrowed as she looked at Jacob. "I'm not happy that you asked Rachel to cut your hair. You should have waited until I had the time."

Jacob hung his head. "I know that now."

"But since you did ask her, and since you promised to pay her for doing it, then you need to make good on that promise." Mom tipped Jacob's chin up so he was looking at her. "I should make you go around with your hair like that until it grows out."

Jacob's eyes got real huge. "Aw, Mom, please, can't you do something to make me look better?"

"I suppose I can try to even it up some." Mom handed the baby to Rachel. "Hannah has a dirty windel, so I'd like you to change it while I trim Jacob's hair."

Rachel wrinkled her nose. "Eww. . .do I have to?"

Mom nodded. "You should be glad I'm not punishing you for cutting your bruder's hair."

"Changing a dirty windel is punishment to me," Rachel mumbled as she carried Hannah out of the room.

On Saturday morning that week, Rachel was headed outside to feed her cats when a blond head appeared around the corner of the barn. It was her English friend Sherry.

"Hi, Rachel," Sherry said. "I came over to see if you could play."

Rachel smiled and lifted the sack of cat food in her hands. "As soon as I feed my cats, I'll be free for the rest of the day."

"Do you need to check with your folks first and see if they want you to do something else?" Sherry asked.

Rachel shook her head. "Mom took Hannah over to my sister Esther's house awhile ago, and she'll probably be gone for several hours. Pap, Henry, and Jacob are working in the fields, so they won't need me."

"What about your grandpa? Will he need your help in the greenhouse?"

Rachel shook her head again. "I don't think so. He hasn't had much for me to do there lately."

"That's too bad. I know how much you like working in the greenhouse," Sherry said.

"I do," Rachel agreed, "but I've been busy with schoolwork and other things."

"I know what you mean. It seems like the older I get, the more homework I have." Sherry shrugged. "Guess it's all part of growing up."

"I suppose so." Rachel started walking for the barn. After the chickens had made a mess on the back porch and had eaten the cats' food, Mom had made Rachel keep the cats' dishes in the barn. She guessed that made sense since Snowball and Cuddles liked to play and sleep in the barn.

"You can help me feed the cats if you want to," Rachel said to Sherry. "When we're done we can think of something fun to do."

"Sounds like a plan." Sherry ran ahead of Rachel and opened the barn door.

When they stepped inside, Cuddles and Snowball darted out from behind a bale of hay and ran toward Rachel.

"Are you hungry?" she asked, pouring food into their bowls.

Meow! Cuddles stuck her head in the dish and started crunching away.

Meow! Snowball did the same.

Sherry snickered. "They act like they haven't been fed in days."

"They've been fed all right." Rachel shrugged. "They always act desperate, and Snowball is a regular sau."

"What's a sau?" Sherry asked.

"It means 'pig.'" Rachel motioned to the cats' dishes. "See what I mean? They've eaten almost all the food I put in."

Sherry laughed. "My dog Bundles eats like a sau, too."

Rachel moved toward the door. "Let's leave these two alone to finish their meal while we find something fun to do."

When they stepped outside, Sherry pointed to the horse and buggy tied to the hitching rail near the barn. "Whose rig is that?" she asked.

"It belongs to my oldest brother, Henry," Rachel said. "He was planning to run to town for some supplies, but Pap asked him to go to the fields to help with something first."

"You know," said Sherry as she continued to stare at the buggy, "I've always wondered what it'd be like to ride in one of those."

Rachel shrugged. "It's nothing special to me, but I've ridden in buggies since I was a baby."

"I'd sure like to take a ride in that buggy," Sherry said wistfully. "Do you think I can?"

Rachel shook her head. "I don't think so. When Henry gets back from helping Pap, he'll be heading for town to run his errands, and I'm sure he won't have time to give you a buggy ride."

"It's not fair," Sherry said. "You got to ride in my brother's car when we went to Hershey Park this summer. I'd really like a ride in that buggy."

"Like I said, it's not possible because—"

"You could give me a ride," Sherry said. "If your brother went to help in the fields, it might be quite awhile before he gets back."

Rachel shook her head vigorously. "No! I've never driven a buggy before."

"Never?"

"Nope."

"But I thought Amish kids learned how to drive a horse and buggy when they were young. That's what my brother, Dave, told me he heard someone say."

"Well, I did sort of drive the buggy once," Rachel said. "It was last summer, and I was sitting on my dad's lap, and he let me hold the reins. I'm not sure I could do it alone, though."

"You'll never know until you try." Sherry touched Rachel's arm. "Would you do it as a favor to me?"

"I—I don't know. . . ."

"Please, Rachel. I know you can do it, and we wouldn't have to go very far. . .just to the end of your driveway and back."

Rachel thought about that. Would it be okay to do as Sherry suggested? They wouldn't go far, and she was pretty sure she could make the horse do what she wanted him to.

"Okay," Rachel said. "I'll take you for a ride down our driveway and back."

"Yeah!" Sherry clapped her hands and jumped up and down. "I can hardly wait!" She tossed her sweater into the buggy and scrambled into the passenger's side on the left.

Rachel untied the horse, backed him away from the hitching rail, and climbed into the buggy on the right side, where the driver was supposed to sit. Then she gathered the reins and clucked to the horse, the way she'd seen Pap do many times.

Clip-clop. Clip-clop. The horse plodded along the driveway. *This is easy,* Rachel thought. *It's actually kind of fun.*

"Can't you make him go faster?" Sherry asked, nudging Rachel's arm.

Rachel snapped the reins, and the horse picked up speed.

"Let's go out on the road," Sherry said.

Rachel shook her head. "No! That could be dangerous."

"It won't hurt anything, Rachel," Sherry said. "You're doing a good job driving the buggy, and we don't have to go very far."

Rachel bit her lower lip. If she could drive the buggy out on the road by herself, she would prove she was grown up.

"Okay, here we go." Rachel guided the horse onto the road and smiled when he did as she directed.

Sherry nudged Rachel's arm again and giggled. "This is sure fun, isn't it?"

Rachel nodded and tried to concentrate on what she was doing.

They'd only gone a short distance when the buggy hit a rut in the road. Sherry's sweater slid off the seat and landed on the floor by Rachel's feet. Rachel leaned to pick it up, and then—*Beep! Beep!*—a car honked its horn as it sped past.

Neigh! Neigh! The horse jerked its head and pulled the buggy straight into a ditch!

Rachel gasped. "Oh no, we're stuck!" She looked over at Sherry. "What are we going to do?"

Chapter 12

A New Opportunity

Sherry clutched Rachel's arm. "Can you get the horse to pull us out of here?"

Rachel leaned out the side opening of the buggy and groaned. "I don't think we'll be going anywhere in this buggy."

"Why not?"

"Looks like the right front wheel is broken."

"Oh, great!" Sherry frowned. "Now what are we going to do?"

"We'd better get out and walk back home to get help." Rachel didn't really want to go ask for help. She knew she'd be in trouble for taking the buggy out, but she had no other choice. She wished she hadn't taken Sherry's advice and driven the buggy. She knew now that it had been a really dumb thing to do.

Rachel and Sherry climbed out of the buggy, and Rachel unhitched the horse.

"What are you doing?" Sherry asked.

"I'm taking the horse with us," Rachel said. "We can't leave him here by himself."

"Oh, okay."

As Rachel turned the horse around and started walking back toward the house, a feeling of dread filled her. She'd really blown it when she'd listened to Sherry's bad advice. She hated to think of the trouble she'd be in, but she couldn't undo what had been done.

The closer Rachel got to home, the more nervous she became. By the time the girls entered the yard, her hands were so sweaty she could barely hang on to the horse's reins.

"Where have you been, Rachel, and what are you doing with that horse?" Pap asked as he, Henry, and Jacob came running out of the barn.

With a shaky voice, Rachel explained what had happened. She ended it by saying, "I'm very sorry, Pap. I know what I did was wrong."

"You're right about that." Pap's face was red, and a muscle on the side of his neck quivered like a bowl of jelly.

"You don't even know how to drive a horse and buggy," Jacob said. "It was sure a dumm thing to do!"

Tears welled in Rachel's eyes. She didn't need her brother's reminder that what she'd done was dumb.

"It was my fault," Sherry spoke up. "I'm the one who wanted to take the buggy ride." She slipped her arm around Rachel's waist. "I talked her into driving the buggy and said I knew she could do it."

Pap looked at Sherry and slowly shook his head. "Asking Rachel to give you a ride was very bad advice." Then he turned to Rachel and said, "You shouldn't have listened to your friend, but I'm glad no one was hurt."

Rachel swallowed the lump in her throat. "I'm glad of that, too."

"The boys and I will see about getting the buggy home now. We'll talk about your punishment when we get back, Rachel." He looked at Sherry again. "You'd better head for home, because Rachel's done playing for the day."

Sherry nodded and hugged Rachel. "I'll see you some other time, Rachel."

"Good-bye, Sherry," Rachel mumbled.

As Rachel headed for the house, she determined that she'd never listen to anyone's bad advice again. From now on she'd try to remember to think things through.

Rachel had just finished making some bologna and cheese sandwiches when Pap came into the house.

"Did you fix the buggy wheel?" Rachel asked.

Pap shook his head. "Had to replace it with a new one." He plunked his hat on the counter and turned to Rachel. "I know that you realize you did wrong by taking the horse and buggy out by yourself. However, you need to be punished so you'll remember not to do such a foolish thing again."

She dropped her gaze to the floor. "Are you gonna give me a bletsching?"

"No, Rachel, but you will have to save your money and pay me back for the buggy wheel I just bought from Audra Burkholder's daed." Pap lifted her chin. "And you won't be allowed to go anywhere but church and school for the next two weeks."

Rachel nodded slowly. She wondered if she would ever grow up and quit doing things that got her into trouble. When she was old and gray, she might still be trying to stay out of trouble.

Pap rested his bearded chin on top of Rachel's head and gave her back a couple of pats. "Now finish getting lunch on the table. The boys and Grandpa will be in soon, and I'm sure they'll want to eat."

"What about Mom?" Rachel asked. "Won't she be coming home for lunch?"

"I don't think so," Pap said. "She told me before she left this morning that she planned to stay at Esther's for most of the day."

"Oh, okay." Rachel reached into the cupboard, took out five plates and five glasses, and placed them on the table. Then she opened a bag of potato chips and put it on the table, along with a jar of dill pickles. She'd just started pouring apple cider into one of the glasses when Grandpa, Jacob, and Henry came into the kitchen.

"What's to eat?" Jacob asked. "I'm hungry as a mule."

"Rachel made some sandwiches." Pap pointed to the sink. "After you wash your hands, we can sit at the table."

The menfolk took turns washing at the sink while Rachel poured the apple juice.

They'd just sat down when the back door flew open and Rudy stepped into the kitchen, holding Hannah and looking quite upset. "Levi," he said to Pap, "your *fraa* [wife] tumbled down our back porch steps, and I'm pretty sure her leg is broken."

Rachel gasped. Henry and Jacob's eyes widened. Pap and Grandpa jumped out of their seats.

"I've already called for help," Rudy said, "and an ambulance is on its way. I came to tell you what had happened so you could call someone for a ride to the hospital."

Pap grabbed his hat and started across the room. "I'll do that right away."

"I'm coming with you," Grandpa said as he followed Pap out the door.

Rudy came over to Rachel and put Hannah in her lap. "I could have left her with Esther, but I figured she's got enough on her hands looking after Ben."

Rachel nodded and stroked her baby sister's soft cheek. "I can watch Hannah. I've done it before, and I'm sure we'll get along okay."

Rudy hesitated a minute; then he rushed out the door.

Rachel looked at Jacob and Henry, hoping one of them would volunteer to help her look after Hannah. They just sat there, shaking their heads and wearing worried expressions.

"We need to ask God to be with Mom and help her to be okay," Rachel said.

Henry nodded. "That's all we can do right now, and praying for Mom's a good thing."

Rachel closed her eyes and bowed her head. *Dear God,* she silently prayed, *Please be with my mamm, and help her to be okay and not be afraid.*

It was almost time to start supper when Pap and Grandpa brought Mom home from the hospital, wearing her left leg in a cast. Mom hobbled in the door using a pair of crutches and sat on the living room sofa.

Rachel rushed over to Mom and sat down beside her. "Is your leg broken? Does it hurt very much? Will you be okay?"

Mom held up her hand and smiled. "Slow down, Rachel. I can only answer one question at a time."

"Sorry, Mom, but I've been so worried about you."

"We all have been," said Henry as he took a seat on the other side of Mom.

"I broke my leg." Mom motioned to her cast. "I'll have to wear this for six weeks, but I'll be fine." She glanced over at Hannah's empty cradle. "Where's the boppli?"

"She's in her crib taking a nap," Rachel said. She reached over and grabbed Mom's hand. "I know you won't be able to do much for the next several weeks, but I promise to take over your chores, even if I have to stay home from school."

"That won't be necessary," Pap said from where he stood across the room. "I'll see if Grandma Yoder can come over during the day, so you'll only be responsible for watching Hannah before and after school."

"And I'll watch her on the weekends," Rachel said.

Pap nodded. "Right."

Rachel smiled. She felt bad about Mom breaking her leg, but she saw this as a new opportunity to show her family that she was growing up. She hoped God would give her the wisdom to make good decisions and help her stay focused on whatever jobs she was required to do.

That evening, after supper was over and Rachel had done the dishes, she sat at the kitchen table with some heavy notebook paper, some pens, glue, and several of her most colorful pressed flowers.

"What are you doing?" Grandpa asked after he'd poured himself a glass of milk and taken a seat across from Rachel.

"I'm making Mom a get-well card," Rachel said.

"I'm going to take it in the living room to her as soon as I'm done."

Grandpa smiled. "I'm sure she'll appreciate the card."

Rachel yawned. "I hope I can get it done before I fall asleep. It's been a long day."

"Would you like me to finish it for you?" Grandpa asked.

She shook her head. "If I'm going to give Mom the card from me, then I need to make it."

"I guess you're right about that." Grandpa pushed his chair away from the table and stood. "I think I'll go to my room and read awhile." He yawned and stretched his arms over his head. "And then I'll be going to bed."

"Okay. See you in the morning, Grandpa."

When Grandpa left the room, Rachel picked up two of the flowers and glued them to the front of the card. Then she added one more flower inside and wrote a poem. When that was done, she covered the card with contact paper, put it in an envelope, and scurried out of the kitchen. She found Mom in the living room, stretched out on the sofa. Pap sat in his recliner, and Henry and Jacob sat on the floor in front of the fireplace, playing checkers.

Rachel knelt in front of the sofa and handed Mom the card. "This is for you."

Mom smiled and opened the envelope. "What

pretty flowers," she said. "Are they some that you pressed?"

Rachel nodded. "I wrote you a poem on the inside, too."

Mom opened the card and read the poem out loud. "While your leg is broken and you're waiting to get well, remember, if you need my help, just ring the little bell."

"That's a very nice poem," Mom said, patting the top of Rachel's head. "But what little bell are you talking about?"

Rachel jumped up and ran to the desk on the other side of the room. She opened the top drawer and removed a bell. She brought it to Mom and said, "I found this in the bottom of my toy box. I used it when Mary and I played school. When you need me for something, just jingle the bell, and I'll come right away."

Mom smiled and took the bell from Rachel. "Danki, that's very thoughtful of you."

"You're welcome." Rachel yawned noisily. "If you don't need me for anything else, I think I'll go to bed."

"Your daed and brieder are here, so I'll be fine," Mom said.

Rachel bent down and hugged Mom. "Gut nacht, Mom. See you in the morning."

For the next few weeks, whenever Rachel wasn't in

school, she kept busy doing the dishes, cooking meals, cleaning house, and taking care of Hannah. She worked hard and was very tired when she went to bed each night, but she was glad she could help Mom.

One Saturday morning, as Rachel started breakfast, Grandpa stepped into the kitchen and hugged her. "Growing up is hard work, isn't it?" he asked.

She nodded and wiped her sweaty forehead with one corner of her apron. "That's for sure, but I think I'm getting there."

Grandpa smiled. "Jah, I think you are, too." He turned toward the door. "I'm going outside now to bring in some more wood for the fireplace, but I should be back before you have breakfast ready."

"Okay, Grandpa."

Rachel hummed as she took a carton of eggs out of the refrigerator. She knew they'd be good and fresh, since she'd been checking each nesting box every day. No more rotten eggs would be brought into this house. At least not as long as Rachel was collecting them.

She was about to crack the first egg into a bowl when the back door swung open and Jacob stepped into the room. "I need Mom."

"What for?" Rachel asked.

"I was helping Grandpa gather some wood, and I got a nasty *schliffer* [splinter] in my thumb." Jacob frowned as he held up his hand.

"Mom's not up yet." Rachel motioned to the closest chair. "Sit down and I'll get that old schliffer out for you."

Jacob shook his head. "No way! I'm not lettin' you dig around in my thumb and cause me all sorts of pain."

"Ach, don't be such a boppli." Rachel marched across the room and opened the cupboard where Mom kept her first-aid supplies. She took out a needle, a pair of tweezers, a bottle of antiseptic, and a bandage. "Now sit down," she said to Jacob. "I'll have that schliffer out of your thumb in no time."

Jacob looked like he didn't believe her, but he sank into the chair and held out his hand.

"Hold still now," Rachel said as she stuck the needle into Jacob's thumb.

"Yeow! That hurts like crazy!" Jacob jerked his hand, and his face turned red.

"I never said it wasn't going to hurt. I just said I could get it out, but you have to hold still." Rachel gritted her teeth as she stared at the splinter sticking halfway out. She was glad she was wearing her glasses. Without them, she'd never be able to see that tiny little piece of wood.

Rachel picked up the tweezers and pulled the splinter right out. "There now, is that better?"

Jacob nodded and blew out his breath. "Danki. You did a good job with that, little ben—" He stopped speaking, gave Rachel a crooked grin, and said, "Guess I can't call you a little bensel anymore. Especially since you've been acting so grown up lately. From now on I think I'll just call you my 'little sister.' How's that sound?"

Rachel smiled. "Sounds good to me. In fact, I feel really good about it."

Henry came into the room then and flopped into the chair on the other side of the table with a groan.

"What's wrong?" Rachel asked.

"I've got a *koppweh* [headache]," he mumbled as he put his head in his hands.

"No problem; I'll get you some aspirin." Rachel jumped up, scooted over to the first-aid cupboard, and took out a bottle of aspirin. "Here you go," she said, handing it to Henry. "This should take away that koppweh."

Henry looked up at her and smiled. "Danki. You're sure growing up, Rachel. You've been a big help around here lately."

"I hope so," she replied.

The teakettle whistled, and steam rose from the spout. Rachel hurried over to the stove. "I'm making a pot of tea this morning, because we're almost out of coffee," she said just as Mom and Pap entered the kitchen. "Will that be okay?"

"It'll be fine," said Mom as she hobbled across the room with her crutches.

Pap pulled out a chair for her. "I wish I didn't have to wear this cumbersome cast," Mom said with a frown. "I feel so helpless, and I'm not much use to anyone right now."

"You only have a few more weeks to wear your cast," Pap said. "Then you can have your old jobs back." He grinned at Rachel. "I'll bet you'll be glad when that happens, huh?"

Rachel shrugged. "I haven't minded helping."

Pap patted Rachel's back while he looked at Mom. "Our Rachel's sure growing up, don't you agree?"

Mom nodded. "She's been a big help to me around here since I broke my leg. She does most of the chores without even being asked, and I appreciate it." She smiled at Rachel and winked. "Why, it won't be long until you're a young woman, ready to make a home of your own."

Pap gave Rachel's shoulder a gentle squeeze. "Even when you do become a woman, you'll always be my little girl."

Rachel grinned and went back to her job of cracking eggs. The thought of always being Pap's little girl didn't bother her at all. In fact, she kind of liked that idea.

Waaa! Waaa!

"It sounds like Hannah's awake," Mom said. "Would someone please get her for me?"

"If someone will take over cracking the eggs, I'll

get Hannah," Rachel said.

"Hand me the bowl, and I'll crack the eggs," Mom said. "That's one job I can easily do from a sitting position."

Rachel set the carton of eggs and the bowl on the table in front of Mom; then she hurried from the room.

When she entered Mom and Pap's bedroom, Hannah was in her crib, kicking her feet and hollering like crazy.

Rachel stepped up to the crib and to her surprise, Hannah stopped crying, reached her chubby arms out to Rachel, and giggled.

She's growing up, Rachel thought. *Just like me.*

Directions for Making Rachel's Pressed Flowers

Things you will need:

Flowers
Newspapers (black and white sections only)
Scissors
Heavy books
Colored pens or pencils
Corrugated cardboard

1. Place flowers between 10 sheets of newspaper. (Note: Put down 5 sheets of newspaper with no flowers on them; then put flowers on 5 separate pieces of newspaper and add more pieces of blank newspaper to the top. The blank newspapers act as blotting paper to take the moisture out of the flowers.) You can put several flowers on one layer, but make sure the flowers don't touch.

2. Place a piece of corrugated cardboard over the newspaper. For each set of flowers you want to press, add layers of newspaper and cardboard.

3. Place several books on top of the stack of cardboard and newspaper.

4. Write down the date you begin pressing the flowers and keep them in a warm, dry room for about 3 weeks. Remove the books and gently separate the flowers from the newspaper. If the flowers feel stiff and dry, they're ready to use. It's a good idea to keep your flowers inside the newspapers with cardboard between them until you're ready to use them. Pressed flowers can be used to decorate bookmarks, postcards, stationery, or scrapbooks. Be creative and have fun!

Other books by Wanda E. Brunstetter

Children's Fiction

RACHEL YODER—ALWAYS TROUBLE SOMEWHERE SERIES

School's Out!
Back to School
Out of Control
New Beginnings
A Happy Heart
Just Plain Foolishness
Jumping to Conclusions
Growing Up

The Wisdom of Solomon

Adult Fiction

INDIANA COUSINS SERIES
SISTERS OF HOLMES COUNTY SERIES
BRIDES OF WEBSTER COUNTY SERIES
DAUGHTERS OF LANCASTER COUNTY SERIES
BRIDES OF LANCASTER COUNTY SERIES

White Christmas Pie

Nonfiction

Wanda E. Brunstetter's Amish Friends Cookbook
Wanda E. Brunstetter's Amish Friends Cookbook Volume 2
The Simple Life

Follow Rachel Yoder in all her adventures: